Loverbar

By

Lizbette Ocasio-Russe

©*2023 by* Lizbette Ocasio-Russe
Flashpoint Publications
First edition June 2023

FLASHPOINT
PUBLICATIONS

D1519199

ISBN 978-1-61929-502-5

Cover Design by AcornGraphics

Editors Sharon Clark and Nat Burns

Publisher's Note:

Acknowledgments

I would like to express the deepest appreciation to my mentors, Dr. Manuel Martínez, Dr. Loretta Collins, and Dr. Olivia Banner whose mentorship and support were critical in my writing journey and the conception of this project.

Dedication

To the Puerto Rican *cuir* community and my chosen family. Adi, Sebastián, Jhoni, *y* Victoria, *les amo y estoy sumamente agradecida por su tiempo, esfuerzo, y pasión.*

Chapter One

Hurricane Karen

Graci scrunches up her face as the fine line of coke shoots up her nose through a chewed-up straw. The sting is worth it. A half a second of minor pain is all it takes to make the detrimental voice in her head stop. And to get the juices flowing.

"What voice?" her friend Alan had asked once. They'd met more than a decade ago when Graci moved from Ponce to San Juan.

"The one that talks shit."

"Oh, honey. I feel you." Graci recalled how Alan flipped the long hair he didn't have, but always pretended to, when a comment merited emphasis.

"Yeah?"

"Yes. I'm guilty of trying to numb the pain once in a while. It helps to give it a name."

"What do you mean?"

"The voice, give it a name. You can't fight what you don't know."

That day Graci named the negative voice in her head Karen.

You suck.

It's Karen. Today, she won't shut up.

You'll never get this article done in time. You're not even a good writer.

"*Cállate.* Shut up. No negativity." Graci shakes her head, sits up straight, and takes a breath.

You can never get anything done. You're just a hopeless procrastinator. Give up.

Graci shakes her hands violently as if trying to expel all of Karen's bad juju through her fingertips. If she can't beat Karen and get her shit together by the time the hurricane hits, she's screwed.

They warn it's not going to be your average storm, but

who can blame the Puerto Rican people for taking the warning with minimal seriousness? Hurricanes are normal, a yearly occurrence. Graci wouldn't usually be so concerned, but she has to pump this piece out before the hurricane knocks out the power and Internet if she wants to get paid. That's the problem with freelance writing— no job security. Normally, she could easily negotiate an extension, but with the impending storm, power and Internet are not guaranteed and neither is communication with the outside world.

She needs that paycheck, not just to pay the bills, but to get her passion project, Loverbar, up and running. Opening your own *cuir*/queer bar is no joke. Licenses, permits,

employees, rent. The checklist is endless, and the impending hurricane threatens to lengthen the process. But it would be worth it to have her space, a space she promises will be for all the *cuir* kids and marginalized motherfuckers that have never known full freedom.

"All right, baby. Time to pump this shit out and get my money." Graci snorts another line.

She rubs her nose, shakes her head, and looks up at the Judy Garland poster on her wall, a vintage promo for *The Wizard of Oz*, her favorite. "Judy gets it. Don't you Judy?" Graci hums the film's iconic song, "Somewhere Over the Rainbow."

The humming turns to singing.

"Somewhere over the rainbow, Loverbar waits for you. And the storm that will hit has passed and we made it through."

She tried writing the article sober earlier that day, but Karen made it impossible.

The line you just took will help. Maybe you should take another one.

"Not today, Satan. I need to get this done." Graci shakes her head.

Get what done? Some mediocre piece of writing that will only prove to your employers what they already suspect. You're no journalist, you're just a junkie.

"No means no." Graci slaps herself a couple of times, walks to her computer, and plops down, fingers at the ready.

Graci hovers her fingers above the keyboard, in with the

good thoughts, out with the bad.

Ugh, why are you so useless? Face it, you're screwed, and now you're broke. Loverbar is never going to open.

"No one cares, Karen. Damn." Graci runs her fingers through her dark-brown hair.

Just one more line. Graci shifts her focus from the still-blank screen to the baggie sitting a few inches away, the chewed-up straw at its side.

Graci leans on the sink as she glides her glossy, hot-pink eyeliner across the entire edge of her left eyelid. Once she is done with both eyelids, she grabs her mascara, twists it open, and curls her lashes upward, the black thickness holding each hair in place.

"*Rebel girl, rebel girl, rebel girl you are the queen of my world...*"

Graci grabs the remote for the speakers and turns Bikini Kill's song up five notches. She struts and gyrates her way to the closet and pulls out a leopard-print, spaghetti strap crop top trimmed with lime green faux fur. She slips the top over her bare breasts and gets to work putting together the rest of her look. Torn fishnets, high-waisted gold shorts, and multi-colored platform shoes complete her outfit. She nods approvingly as she admires herself in the standing mirror.

The phone rings. Graci answers it. It's Alan.

"*Hola, mi amor*! *Nada*, just getting ready. You're ready for tonight, *¿sí*? No, not yet, but I'm almost done." Graci looks at the blank screen with the cursor blinking, winking, taunting. "Yeah, I can bang out the article in the AM, if need be. It'll get done. Plus, this night is about Lola, the queen of queens! Are you ready for the drag show? What time are we meeting again? Okay, we have to be the loudest ones to make sure Lola gets that title. Ms. *Cuir* Puerto Rico, here we come!

Graci hangs up the phone and walks to the computer. She takes one more look at the screen before slamming it shut. She imagines the cursor bleeding, crushed to death by the force, and smirks as she heads out the door.

The club is overflowing with young flesh as Graci strolls up. Alan is waiting patiently by the small, uneven door staring enthusiastically into his phone. The bouncer standing behind Alan is statuesque, his arms crossed and muscles bulging. Graci always thought the bouncer looked like a roided-out troll guarding a bridge that led to the magical land of booze, babes, and blow. Cigarette butts, roaches, and cans litter the sidewalk. It also smells like hot piss. Graci gags at the rancid odor. She picks up the pace to escape the stench. Loverbar won't smell like this.

"¡*Amor*! Who is demanding your attention now?" Graci says, strutting toward Alan.

Alan looks up, revealing his usual flawless face. His hair is perfectly coiffed and tinged with the latest trending shade of gray, eyes ablaze with silver glitter.

"Oh, just Lola with her excuses. She'll be late to the show, we should move her to the second if not third slot." Alan rolls his eyes.

"That's no biggie, right? Also, nothing new?"

Alan sighs. "Well, it wouldn't be except our first two performers are also late."

"Well, I guess that means we have plenty of time for a drink...or two." Graci grabs Alan's arm and strolls past the troll and across the bridge into wonderland.

The club is a barrage of sweaty bodies breathing and writhing to the beat of indiscriminate Latin-trap. Neon lights of varying pinks, purples, and blues momentarily highlight the individual faces that compose the hoard hoping for happiness night after night, drink after drink, line after line. Graci drags Alan to the bar and orders two vodkas with pink grapefruit. She made sure to specify. The white grapefruit made her gag.

The bartender plops down their drinks, glistening with condensation. Graci wastes no time in snagging hers.

"Thirsty, are we?" Alan watches as Graci knocks back half of her drink.

"Always. Cheers." Graci raises her glass.

Alan grabs his drink and touches it to Graci's.

"So, if we have no queens on deck, I guess I can DJ until Lola decides to grace us with her presence," Graci says.

"Yeah, I don't know. You were kind of a dick last time."

"Oh, please. I wasn't that bad." Graci takes another swig of her drink.

"Understatement of the year." Alan stirs his drink slowly.

"Why don't you focus on just watching and having a good time?"

"*Ay*, relax, you get too stressed when we have an event."

"And you don't get stressed enough," Alan says, still focused on stirring his drink. "I hope you get more stressed about opening Loverbar than you do about these events."

Alan's suggestive tone made Graci's chest sting. She narrows her eyes, glares at Alan, and stalks off.

The club owner relents to letting Graci DJ in less than five minutes, especially considering the promise of a potential blowjob after the night is done.

Graci bobs her head as she breezes through the provided computer's music playlist. It's not much, but she can work with it. Graci digs through her latest thrift store purchase purse and removes a cord which she connects to her phone and then the computer. Beads of sweat slide down Graci's forehead as she dances and adds songs to the queue. The crowd bounces with her, taking every cue she delivers. The look of pleasant surprise on their faces when she drops an old-school reggaeton track gives her goosebumps. Grateful fans bring her drink after drink, shot after shot.

The night passes in a haze of neon lights, smoke, drinks, random make-outs, and nags from Alan.

"The queens are here. You're done." Alan tugs at her arm.

Graci did not notice Alan walk up with the house DJ. She yanks her arm away.

"Okay, okay, *coño, relájate.*"

"*Mala mía.*" Alan brings his fingertips to his temple, closes his eyes, and takes a deep breath. "The first performer is ready for her cue, please, let Juan take it."

"Let this song finish." Graci turns to face the crowd again.

Alan grabs Graci and pulls her away from the DJ booth.

"Don't touch me!" Graci yanks herself out of Alan's grip.

"Graci, *en serio*? That's enough!" Alan gives the DJ a look.

Both Alan and the DJ take hold of Graci who immediately thrashes. The crowd, now taking notice of the scene, stops dancing and focuses its attention on the scuffle.

"Let go, *pendejos*, don't touch me!" With one final emphatic pull, Graci gets out of their grip, trips, and falls onto the computer delivering the beats.

The music stops as the computer and Graci crash to the floor. She tries to get up but wobbles and falls back down. The crowd is silent as the house DJ scrambles to recover the computer and Graci struggles to stand. Alan is wide-eyed shaking his head at Graci sprawled out on the floor drenched in the drink that went flying out of her hand.

Graci scrunches her closed eyes at the pressure of urine filling her bladder. Her face is mashed against the sticky, tiled floor of her one-bedroom Rio Piedras apartment. She hadn't even made it to her bed. She lay, spread eagled on the floor with a half-eaten sandwich to her left and the spilled contents of her purse to the right.

Graci pushes herself off the ground into a seated position. She can feel the make-up and filth from the night before caked onto her greasy face and sweaty body. The sun pouring in through the window causes her to look away. Her hand searches the ground to her right finding everything from coins, empty baggies, lipstick tubes, condoms, and lighters. It's a few seconds before she finds her phone.

Five missed calls, eight texts, all from Lola, Alan, and her mother. Graci rolls her eyes. All the messages are pretty much the same.

Hey, did you get the article done? Let me know you're okay. Te amo.

There's also a voicemail from Lola.

What the fuck, Graci? You almost ruined the show. I lost, not that you care.

Droplets emerge at the corners of Graci's eyes.

You're a terrible friend. No one can rely on you. You keep letting everyone down. Won't you ever learn? Evidently not.

Graci wipes away the tears with a grunt and clears her throat. She types back her generic response of *I'm good, thanks for asking. I got this, no worries.* Then she notices the time. It's noon.

How are you going to get this article done and go shop-

ping for supplies before the hurricane hits? You really messed up this time. You failed as a friend, and now you're failing at work and as an adult.*

"*Ay ya*, it's not like I fell on purpose, and I still have time to finish writing."

She didn't even bother looking at the rest of the messages before busting out her computer.

I can't believe you left shopping for the day of the hurricane. What are you, stupid and *irresponsible? The stores are going to be packed and impossible. You're so pathetic. Loverbar is doomed.*

"Screw you, Karen." Graci uses both hands to flip off her self-deprecation.

Graci's hands make their way down to the keyboard. They tremble as she holds them above the keys. Her knee bounces up and down, up and down.

You're a waste of space. Why try if you already know you're going to fail? It's a statistical fact at this point.

Graci's head is throbbing. She runs her fingers through her hair, stands up, and heads to the fridge.

"Hair of the dog it is."

She pulls out a half-filled bottle of wine, uncorks it with her teeth, chugs the entire thing, and searches the fridge for more.

Her phone buzzes

Graci peels her face off the keyboard which has left small, square imprints on her right cheek. Her mouth is dry, and her head seems to have its own heartbeat. The cursor she had believed to be dead is blinking, blinking, blinking at her from the screen, which is no longer blank, but by no means full. Graci got about a paragraph done and passed out.

Her phone buzzes again. Graci picks it up. It's Alan.

"Lola *está bien molesta*. She is really pissed."

Graci feels her stomach turn.

Yes, you made a scene. Always the drama queen, always selfish.

To make things worse, the clock now reads five in the evening, rush hour the day before the hurricane is supposed to hit. She ends up spending two hours going to and from the grocery store and is unable to find everything she needs.

You knew this would happen. It's your fault for pro-crastinating again. You're so lazy, so useless.

Her only hope for finishing her article on time is this storm having a limp dick, unable to get it up and fuck the shit out of this small Caribbean island.

The interminable sound of the hurricane makes her hair stand on end. It is shrieking, pounding, thundering, banging, every terrifying sound all at once. There's no escaping the noise. It's everywhere, outside and inside her head. Graci sits in the corner of her bathroom, the safest place in her apartment, gritting her teeth.

"It'll pass." She takes swigs from the bottle of rum she got at the store, a replacement for the lack of canned goods and water she missed out on for going to the store so late.

The storm kit she prepared consists of headphones, a lighter, a bag of Doritos, and liquor, lots of liquor. She plugs the headphones into her phone. It has forty percent battery.

"*Mierda.*"

You should've charged it before this went down. And the article, you screwed that one up good, didn't you?

Graci shoves the buds into her ears and presses play. Tears escape despite how tightly she strains to keep them in. "Blitzkrieg Bop" by The Ramones explodes into her ears, but Joey Ramone's voice is not enough to drown out the infernal shrieking of the one hundred seventy-five mile per hour wind outside. Graci takes a swig from the bottle and then another and another until the wind, Joey Ramone, and Karen are silenced.

Graci wakes up, her head throbbing. She stumbles to her feet and accidentally kicks the empty rum bottle which rattles and clanks across the bathroom floor. A serious case of cottonmouth leads her to the sink. She turns the knob, but nothing comes out. She turns both knobs to no avail. Her phone isn't far. It's at one percent battery. She should text Lola.

"Baby, I'm so sorry." Graci pushes send but the screen goes dark. "Shit!" Graci throws the phone down.

She tries to push the door open, but it runs into a blockage with a thud. Graci has drunk herself through the storm.

She keeps pushing the door and is eventually able to squeeze through. Graci tumbles out of her bathroom and takes in her apartment. The floor is soaked. It seeped in under the front door and through the broken window sitting next to it. Luckily, the door and windows have bars that prevented large debris from finding its way in, but the furniture is ruined. The bed is soaked and covered in dirt and leaves that were forced through the windows. Her once colorful walls of retro posters, neon signs, and pictures are practically bare. The few items left hanging are tattered or broken, scarcely clinging to the wall. Among the survivors is *The Wizard of Oz* poster. It's wet, frayed, and torn down the middle. The hurricane ripped Dorothy right in half.

Graci slowly makes her way outside where people are walking around aimlessly. They look around wide-eyed, some mouths agape, some mouths covered. Some people are already clearing garages and streets that are completely blocked with fallen trees, telephone poles, jacked-up vehicles, furniture, everything imaginable. Graci's heart palpitates as she takes in the roofless houses, strewn vehicles, and flooded streets that have made the neighborhood unrecognizable. The familiar faces of the homeless that often settle on her street are nowhere to be found. The sound of children crying is the worst.

A drizzle begins as Graci stumbles down the street. She trips on a lamp post but manages to stay on her feet. She has to check on the location for Loverbar.

"*Ay, m'ija, gracias a Dios.* Thank goodness, you're okay." Graci's elderly neighbor is shuffling to her, waving her hands to the heavens in gratitude.

She is always concerned about Graci.

"I tried to find you before the storm, but you never answered the door."

"Oh, well...I must have been at the store. I'm glad you're all right. Let me know if you need anything."

The elderly lady waves away the offer, smiling.

"I'll be just fine, tough as nails, just like *mi mamá, Dios la cuide.*" She crosses herself. "If you need something, you know where to find me."

The neighbor begins to walk away but turns and looks Graci up and down.

"*Te ves malita.* You look ill...if you need anything at all, *m'ija*, please, don't hesitate."

"I'm fine, really, but thank you." Graci waves goodbye.

Graci continues down the street toward the location of Loverbar.

The space is going to be a disaster. Everything flooded, broken, and ruined. Just like you.

Graci shakes her head but fails to shake Karen. A pit emerges and begins widening in her stomach. She's just over-reacting, right? Everything will be fine. It has to be. When she arrives at the location, the surrounding area is covered in debris, but the building seems mostly unscathed compared to the businesses around it. The awning is torn off and is nowhere in sight, but the door is not blown off. Maybe it won't be too bad inside.

A week later, it's clear help isn't coming. People create their own rescue and clearance teams to remove the debris blocking roads and houses. Graci, Alan, Lola, and others from the *cuir* community organized their own rescue team which planned to not only clear roads but also spread emergency supplies and offer food to those in need.

"You're ready for tomorrow, right? You're picking me up at seven in the morning. Sharp. We are going to my hometown. I can't be late." Alan's voice is stern.

"*Aja.* Yes, Sergeant Alan, chill," Graci says, while arranging lines on her desk. Her ATM card cuts expertly through the coke, arranging four perfect lines.

"*Graci, en serio.*"

"*Si, nene, Dios mío*, chill out. I'll be there. Do I need to pick Lola up?"

"No, she's riding with someone else."

Graci snorts the first line, no straw this time, just raw nostril. She twitches and sniffles loudly, startling herself. She has executed the action silently so many times, that her audible reaction to the sharp powder is more confusing than shocking.

"What was that?"

"Nothing. I'll see you tomorrow, okay?" Graci hangs up by slamming the phone.

She looks around her apartment now dry but no less disheveled from last week's storm. The damage, usually a stressor, is a pleasant distraction from Alan's misplaced concern. Her window is still broken, but she has a roof. She should be grateful. Houses down the street are missing doors, windows, roofs, and some are irreparably crushed by trees, telephone poles, and large debris. Graci catches her reflection on what's left of the window. She fixes on the sight of herself huddled above the remaining lines of coke.

Not even your best friend trusts you. Alan knows exactly what you are, a selfish, useless junkie.

Graci snorts a second line.

You should just call Alan back and tell him that you won't be there. But you can't even do that, can you? You can't even be honest with your best friend. You can't even ask for help. You deserve everything you get.

Graci snorts the last two lines back-to-back.

"*Déjame quieta*, Karen. Leave me alone. Dear goddess in heaven, if you exist, please make her go away. Whatever divinity exists, do me a solid just this once."

Graci made her way to the fridge. She grabs the bottle of rum sitting next to it and searches inside for a mixer. There's half a gallon of water, two apples, a soy sauce-stained carton of Chinese food, an onion, and half a bottle of Coke. She grabs the Coke and unscrews the cap foolishly hoping for fizzing indicating remnant carbonation. Nothing. Graci fills the rest of the Coke bottle to the brim with rum and takes a long, hard, swig.

Graci slowly opens her eyes and lifts her head from the puddle she has been laying in. Graci leans down and takes a whiff. No gag, so it's not urine or puke. Instead, the smell of stale sugar. Graci looks around for her phone, she spots it under the couch. Upon inspection, she sees ten missed calls, all from Alan.

"*Sea la madre*, they're going to kill me."

Graci tries to call Alan but fumbles with the phone. It falls to the ground and turns off.

"Fuck's sake."

After a few minutes, Graci manages to get the phone on. There's a new voicemail from Alan.

"I don't know what happened, but please call me and let me know you're okay. I'm worried about you."

Although the concern is evident in his voice, his tone is laced with anger. Graci throws her phone across the room. It shatters on the wall. The bottle of rum is empty. She feels her face grow hot and her hands tremble. She searches the apartment. Her forehead breaks into a sweat as she rummages through purses, pants pockets, pantries, and the fridge. No baggies, no booze. Nothing.

"*Damn it!*" Graci slams the wall with her palms.

The bathroom.

Graci rushes into the bathroom. She grabs the mouthwash, unscrews the cap, and chugs.

Chapter Two

That was then, this is now

"Graci, *por favor*, I beg you, please come to Orlando until this gets better. How can you work *sin electricidad*, without power?"

Graci rolls her eyes at her mother's plea. She has cousins in Florida that offered her and her mother a place to stay until conditions on the island improve. It's been four months since Hurricane María hit and the island is nowhere near recovered. Graci takes a deep breath in, filling her belly with air instead of emptying it. This is what last night's meditation video on ocean breathing taught her. It's called the Ujjayi breath, or ocean breath, and is supposed to calm the mind and warm the body. Not that Graci needs any help warming up. No power means no AC or fans. Damp flesh dripping with thick drops of salty perspiration is the new normal.

"*Mami*, no. I'm not coming home. I can't just leave my friends." Graci wipes her brow and flicks off the sweat threatening to trickle into her eyes.

"*¿Cómo que no*? This is about your safety and wellbeing! Mi amor, por favor, you can't take care of other people until you've—"

Graci hangs up before her mother has a chance to finish. She throws the new phone into the hot pink futon sitting across the room and lets her head fall into her hands. She takes another deep breath in, and out, in, and out, just like the ocean, just like the ocean.

"Crap." Graci looks at the Wonder Woman watch she always chooses to wear instead of the Cartier her mother gave her for her thirtieth birthday the year before.

She bought it the day she decided to get sober believing that the cartoon amazon flexing her divine muscles on the red, plastic surface would be a good grounding mechanism when the itch became too much.

Graci can't be late. She hasn't been late in two months, and she's not going to start now. Once Graci leaves the apartment, no service is guaranteed. Despite months having passed since Hurricane María, water, power, and groceries are still a rarity. She quickly gives herself a glance in the standing mirror by the futon, grabs her zebra-print purse, shoves her wallet and phone into it, and rushes out the door.

Graci can't help but notice how much clearer the streets are now. Not that the government did much to make that happen. People had to take things into their own hands. Graci's neighborhood was practically inaccessible until she and other neighbors decided to clear the streets themselves. Trees, telephone poles, and miscellaneous debris galore kept them busy for days, weeks.

The first day she began helping clear the streets was a bit rough. Graci thinks of Alan's face that day as she arrived late. It was the first time she had seen Alan so quiet. To be fair, it was her own hungover ass's fault. She deserved all the shit she got.

"*Mis amores, por favor*, I'm so, so sorry. I know I fucked up—I've fucked up too many times."

Alan and Lola refused to look her in the eye.

"Words mean shit, I know that. I'll show you. Starting today." Graci sighed deeply, removing her sunglasses.

The dark bags under her bloodshot eyes extended to her cheekbone, she looked Alan in the eye.

"*Ya verás.*"

She smiled at the memory, but it's quickly replaced by a furrowed brow and down-turned lips. She can't tell anyone until she's at least three months clean. Action, not words. Two down, one to go.

Graci continues walking down the Avenida de la Constitución until she spots her scarcely started business, Loverbar, *un lugar para todes*, a place for all. All it has so far is a name and location. She must stay sober for her future business, too many people are counting on it. It's the *cuir* space everyone needs. At first, Hurricane María seemed like the worst thing that could happen to her up-and-coming business, all renovation was forced into an indefinite hold. But if the hurricane wouldn't have happened, the opening of Loverbar would have proceeded as scheduled, and she would've driven that shit to the ground.

But, today, it isn't about clearing the streets, it's about feeding the people. The crew is meeting with Graci to plan their next communal meal.

They did not have much choice when choosing a place to meet. Of course, the only place in the neighborhood with power is a bar. Tonee's to be exact. Graci has spent many a drunken night there, most of which she does not fully remember. BecauseTonee's the bar is right in the middle of the neighborhood and has electricity, it's become the go-to meet-up spot for the peeps of Rio Piedras. A jacked-up power grid equals zero cell service so getting in touch with others is impossible. Graci gets spotty service occasionally, but others, like her friend Valeria, get nothing all day.

It's almost six when Graci arrives at Tonee's, and there's already a crowd beginning to form. She stops and takes it in. A small crowd would have terrified her a few weeks back. It was terrible just waiting and waiting for her friends to show up that first day. After she had found Alan, it took an hour to find Lola.

Graci couldn't keep from imagining the worst as she searched for Lola. Was she crushed by a collapsed roof, swept away in the flood, trapped by debris? It made her itch, that familiar itch that can only be pacified with a minimum of five percent alcohol volume.

Graci shakes the memory away. That was then, this is now. She's got this. She takes a deep breath and heads toward the small but growing crowd in front of Tonee's. Inside, there are more people taking full advantage of the AC and unreliable but available Wi-Fi and cell service. All the tables are practically full of both people and beer cans. Hell, if there is no water, drink beer. It did keep everyone alive in medieval times because of the risk of sepsis and whatever...right?

Graci made her way to the bar, slows down as she approaches it.

"*Permiso.*" A stranger shoves past her and takes a spot at the bar. "*Una Medalla, porfa.*"

"*Están caliente*, they are warm," the bartender says, while breaking a twenty with large but agile hands.

The stranger waves off the comment. Warm beer is better than no beer.

Graci waits until the stranger vacates the spot and made her move. The bartender looks at her expectantly. She places her hands on the bar top and spots the cooler behind the bartender packed with rows and rows of beer. It does not have the variety it used to have before Hurricane María, as supplies island-wide have waned, but it still holds the tried-and-true brands whose popularity assures their availability including Michelob, Heineken, Corona, and the island's own, Medalla. Condensation is beginning to form on a few cans.

They must be starting to cool down.

"Which one do you want?" the bartender says, noticing Graci's gaze fixed on the cooler.

Graci does not budge, she does not speak, she only stares, her fingertips now white from gripping the bar top.

"Hey...*mira!*" The bartender snaps his fingers a few inches from Graci's face.

"Oh, ah, *mala mía*, my bad. Can I just get a—"

"Coronas are the coldest right now." He reaches into the cooler, pulls one out, and places it in front of Graci.

For a second, she is frozen. Her right hand twitches for a moment as if making to grab the bottle but she spots her Wonder Woman watch and keeps her hand glued to the bar. She takes a deep breath, closing her eyes. All she has to do is order a water and keep her eyes closed until that beer is gone.

Open your eyes. You know you want to.

****

Lola and Alan arrive and snag a table. When Alan spots Graci by the bar, he immediately tenses up.

"*Vengo ahora*, I'll be right back." Alan leaves the table and makes his way to Graci.

His eyes widen as he shoves his way through the crowd. Making his way to Graci is proving difficult.

"Oh, my gawd!" An individual dressed in skin-tight white jeans, a fuchsia button-down, and some fresh black dress shoes drapes his arms over Alan's shoulders, drawing the last word out.

Alan's legs buckle slightly under the weight.

Alan shoves him off. "Ew, what the hell?"

The drunkard stumbles a bit but keeps smiling, nonetheless. Alan rolls his eyes upon recognition.

"Get your shit together, Nelson." Alan shakes his head trying not to recall the misguided evening he made out with that fool.

Graci is only a few feet away. One, two, three awkward gropes later, Alan is closing in on Graci. He sees a Corona sweating deliciously before her and feels his stomach drop.

****

Unaware of Alan behind her, Graci's eyes remain closed, but they jolt open when a disembodied hand clamps down on her shoulder.

"Are you seriously going to drink now? We have shit to figure out."

Graci whips around to find Alan looking like Lola when she walked in on her fiancé whipping her cousin Gabriel to the point of ecstasy.

"That's not mine. I didn't—"

"*Si*, okay, just like when it wasn't a blackout hangover that kept you from making it to our first street clean on time."

Graci goes to speak but holds her tongue and stalks off toward Lola who is saving the table. Alan follows. Graci and Alan take a seat avoiding each other's gaze.

"Okay, so what's the plan?" Graci sits upright in her chair, her posture perfect. In addition to practicing the Ujjayi breath, Graci's meditation videos before the hurricane had insisted that sitting and walking with your back straight and in alignment helps keep your mind and soul in alignment as well.

After the rest of the crew arrives, they decide they will each fan out and find three people that need a place to eat this week. The communal meal is to be prepared and served at Graci's neighbor's house, where she is currently house sitting. The crew will split the grocery list, go to the grocery store together, spread out, and shop. The limits set for certain grocery items make shopping impossible, so they need to shop individually to be able to get as many items as possible.

But who can blame the stores for trying to prevent selfish assholes from hoarding? Going to the supermarket these days is like participating in a game of capture the flag with no teams or rules. Every person for themself. The flags are the coveted grocery items, a true commodity on an island, and the employees are the referees ensuring people do not get too greedy. Of course, the employees would not think the crew greedy if they knew they were shopping for multiple people.

Graci prepares for the expedition while waiting for the mobile banking app to load on her phone. Cell service has gotten significantly worse since yesterday when she last spoke to her mother. It's a bit of a relief knowing she won't have to stomach Mami begging her to join her in Orlando today, but that also means she will not know if her mother sent some cash unless she can get into her bank account.

At first, Graci could not handle the help.

"A thirty-year-old woman should be able to take care of herself," Graci said when her mother first insisted on helping her financially after Hurricane María made working impossible.

But hunger sucks, and, eventually, Graci caved.

"You have to know when to ask for and accept help." This comment from her mother did not help. "Especially from your parents. Graci, being able to help you is—Well, it's everything." This comment helped.

The banking app is still loading. Graci takes in her reflection—red high-waisted shorts, a Black Lives Matter T-shirt, white-fringed boots, and a rainbow purse. Just because everything else looks like crap does not mean she has to.

Graci turns to the side and admires her profile once more before shifting her attention to the phone. She tosses the rainbow purse on the hot pink futon. A small, plastic baggie falls from the open zipper. There's no way there's anything in there.

Graci grabs the baggie with a trembling hand, drops it immediately, and closes her eyes. Graci turns away from where she let the thing fall and bends down, feeling around for her phone. Okay, when she opens her eyes, she's going to check her phone and go. Alan will be outside any minute, she'll deal with this later. One, two, three.

Graci opens her eyes. The bank app is not done loading.

Damn. The phone begins to tremble in her hands. She grips it tighter and closes her eyes. Immediately, she's bombarded with unflattering yet inviting images of herself just a few weeks ago, passed out in a puddle of her own sick in the living room, wandering the streets at three in the morning in search of a fix, blowing a random guy in a random bathroom for the sake of some blow.

Just open your eyes and get it done. You're going to break eventually.

Graci shakes her head, but Karen is not easily dissuaded. Afraid more images of her past will come pouring in, Graci opens her eyes. The powdery devil stares, taunts, calls. Her hand seems to belong to another as it made its way to the baggie. Graci watches helplessly.

There's a knock on the door.

Graci jumps, her hand retreating, a frightened white rabbit scurrying back to its burrow.

"Graci." It's Alan. "Are you ready? I've been waiting outside for ten minutes."

Graci grabs her purse and heads to the door, checking her phone in the process. The app is done loading.

"Yes. Thank you, Mom."

She should tell Alan. Should she tell Alan? Maybe she shouldn't tell Alan.

Graci strolls down aisle four doing her best not to bump into anyone, but people are running around, shoving, and snatching groceries like it's a sport. She is tasked with getting the rice and beans, two of the most difficult items to snag.

Alan won't believe she's been sober. He will just make things worse, just like this idiot trying to hog all those cans of beans. Are you kidding me? Graci waits for a gap in the crowd of people around the rice and beans. She sighs, rolling her eyes as people continue to clutter and clammer. After a few seconds, Graci shoves into the crowd and does not stop until she reaches the front. No eye contact, no apologies. She manages to get three cans, which is the limit. The rice is on the bottom shelf but bending down is impossible when she's sandwiched like this. Remembering her more hardcore punk days, Graci gives two powerful shoves in either direction and drops to the floor.

Alan just wants to help. She should just—ouch, *coño*! Graci pulls her hand out from under the shoe that crushed it and immediately goes for the nearest bag of rice. Success!

She crawls out of the throng and stands up smoothing out her skirt and shirt.

Animals.

Graci stumbles through her front door releasing the groceries onto the ground with a grunt. She pretends she does not remember the baggie of cocaine sitting on her futon and focuses on putting the plastic grocery bags away for recycling and filling her tote bags in preparation for transporting the groceries to the neighbor's place. When she's done, a magnetic force pulls her toward the futon. Graci walks toward the bathroom attempting to wash her face and get her shit together but veers off course toward the baggie lying on the futon.

Just a little bit won't make a difference. If anything, it'll make you more present, enjoy the moment and shit. You're only young once...

Her hand reaches out, takes the baggie, and spills out the contents. Graci retrieves a card from her wallet and begins cutting lines. She can't stop it, there's no convincing her body to release the card and move away from the coke.

The alarm on her Wonder Woman watch goes off, indicating it's time to make her way to the neighbor's house and begin preparing for their guests' arrival. Graci freezes and begins to shake. She looks at the watch then at the hand holding the card.

"Let go." Graci's hand obeys and releases its grip.

The card falls to the floor, scattering the lines. Graci pops up into a standing position, her chest heaving.

"Get it together." Graci slaps herself across the face and hurries into the bathroom.

The cold water feels heavenly on her hot face. She holds her face under the running water for a moment, gives herself a good scrub, and rushes out making sure to avoid eye contact with the white devil.

Twenty-five people show up at Graci's neighbor's house for the communal meal. Her neighbor's place became like a second home after Graci showed up a crying mess asking for help. The elderly woman did not ask questions and immediately invited Graci to stay with her until she was better. That's exactly what Graci did. So, when the elderly lady took off to Florida after the hurricane, she left the place to Graci.

"This is the biggest turn-out we've had." Graci closes the gate behind the last guest. "We done good."

Alan watches from the doorway, leaning on the frame, a smile creeping onto his face.

"Let's not celebrate just yet," Alan says, gesturing into the house. "We still need to cook dinner for twenty-five people without poisoning them or burning the house down."

"Okay, Debbie Downer, gawd." Graci rolls her eyes but smiled as she heads inside.

Alan stops her.

"Hey, I'm proud of you. This—" Alan leads her into the house and kitchen.

Everyone is gathered around the kitchen island sharing the warm water and juice they managed to get at the store.

"You did this despite—well, you did this. You should be proud."

Graci's eyes meet his for a second. What? No sarcasm? No judgment? She searches and searches, but no red flags.

"I guess we should get to it then."

Lola takes charge of the rice and beans, which she brags her grandmother taught her to cook to perfection, while Alan takes care of the plantains. *Tostones* are his specialty. Graci focuses on her usual potato salad. She's rarely proud to be a quarter white, but her grandmother's potato salad recipe is an American delicacy she is glad to have inherited. It got her many compliments and praise at birthday and holiday parties. The best part about this entire meal was the high-calorie count.

"How long has it been for you?" Lola asks one of the guests, Ash, while filling the pot with water.

"How long what? An actual meal? Like a month."

Lola almost drops the pot into the sink. "Honey, what have you been eating?"

"Mostly bread, chips, and ramen when I can get some."

They sit around the table with the meal prepped and served. The beans are still in the pot, steam rising, fumes expanding. The smell seems to have the same effect on everyone. Tense faces loosen and eventually relax into a primitive smile that says yum.

"Maybe someone should say a prayer," Lola says.

Everyone at the table whips their head around to face Lola, eyes wide, eyebrows raised.

"Since when are you religious?" Alan says.

Lola throws her hands up surrendering to their attack.

"Ay, ya! Sorry for being grateful. It's not like I'm going to run to confession, I'm just trying to acknowledge," Lola points to the food and people gathered. "That this is fucking amazing."

"You're right," Alan says. "*Mala mía*, my bad. That was bitchy of me."

"I'll do it," Graci says.

Everyone turns to look at her.

"*En el nombre del Padre, del Hijo, y del Espíritu Santo.* In the name of the Father, the Son, and the Holy Spirit."

Everyone traces their right hand from their forehead to their belly button to their left shoulder and finally to their right shoulder, this knowledge not a sign of their devotion to God but of their being raised to praise.

"Thank you for us—for this. It's been a challenge, to say the least. María was a bitch to us so now we have to deal with her mess in addition to our own. But screw it. We got this. We've handled shit before, we'll handle it again. That's why we're here, that's why this is possible."

Alan squeezes Graci's hand. She continues. "Bless the hands that prepared this meal and those that will receive it and allow us to continue helping those the government ignores. Before we eat, why don't we take a moment of silence for all of those that lost their lives because of the storm."

Everyone remains silent for a few seconds.

"Thank you everyone for being here, there will always be

a warm meal and a place to stay with me if you need it. Oh— Amen."

Everyone crosses themselves and opens their eyes. Some eyes are watering.

"Hemingway, I'm overcome here," Alan says, wiping a tear from his eye.

A few half-hearted chuckles and sniffles, all good.

Lola claps her hands twice, effectively snapping everyone out of their consuming thought. "All right, enough mush. Let's eat."

The kitchen counter is covered with dishes, pots, pans, utensils, and cups. Graci takes the first washing shift allowing the others to chat a bit more as they enjoy their drinks. She tackles the plates first, circular motion after circular motion. It's a very meditative practice if you have the right mindset. Most people only wax on when washing plates, constant circular motions to the left. Ever since Graci watched the *Karate Kid* when she was six years old, she decided it best to wax both on and off if only for the sake of balance. Balance, after all, is everything, according to Mr. Miyagi.

A pair of hands slide around her waist until meeting at her belly button.

"I'm so proud of you, baby," Alan says, nuzzling her cheek from behind.

Graci does not turn around and continues washing.

"*Ay, por favor*. This wasn't just me."

"True, but it was mostly you."

She should tell him.

"Alan, there's something I have to tell you."

Alan releases Graci, the tone of her voice bringing him to seriousness. Alan waits.

"Would you just—come with me?"

Alan studies Graci, then relents. The pair excuse themselves from the dinner guests and make their way next door to Graci's apartment.

"You're scaring me. What's going on?" Alan says, once they are a few steps from Graci's front door.

Graci looks at Alan, drops her gaze, and opens the door.

"On the floor by the couch—I didn't know what to do."

Alan walks into the apartment and made his way to the

coke strewn on the floor. Graci rubs her right arm and breathes a bit heavier.

Alan takes a deep breath, picks up the baggie, and turns to face Graci.

"Did you take any? Is that why you were all inspired and shit during that prayer?"

Graci's eyes grow glassy. "Jesus, no, please—just—"

"Because I can't deal with this anymore." Alan stalks into the bathroom, empties the contents of the baggie into the toilet, and flushes it.

"Will you stop making me feel like shit."

Alan takes a step back, eyes wide. Graci collapses, breaking down into a mess of tears and snot.

"I'm trying to tell you I need help with this." Graci's body heaves as she speaks through sobs. "It's been two months, I didn't want to say anything until I hit the three-month mark, but I'm scared I won't make it."

Alan sits next to Graci on the floor and places an arm around her.

"The other night at Tonee's. You didn't order that beer?"

"No. I swear. And then today when you got here to pick me up that fell out of my purse."

Alan looks down and sighs.

"I'm so sorry, Alan. I should've told you or anyone. But I didn't take anything, I didn't drink anything. I swear, I swear!" Graci continues sobbing, that familiar itch spreading inside of her, begging for sweet relief.

Alan looks up at Graci and takes her face in his hands. He looks into her eyes, studying. "*Mi amor*, I believe you, and I'm proud of you."

"Really?" Graci collapses into her best friend's arms.

"Two months already? That's huge. Also, asking for help is not easy, especially when people can be judgmental dicks. I'm sorry."

After Graci takes a moment to get herself together, the two rejoin everyone at dinner.

"Where have y'all been? Damn." Lola is busy doing the dishes.

She stops when she notices Graci's red eyes and Alan's soft smile.

"What's wrong, what happened?" Lola says, searching both Alan and Graci's faces.

"Graci has some good news."

Chapter Three

Pinky's Box

Pinky is putting the finishing touches on her makeup when her phone rings.

"Hey, beautiful. Do you have plans today?" It's Graci. She never misses a drag show, but she's kind of a drunken mess.

Regardless, Pinky loves her. Graci was there when Pinky came out and got kicked out of her parents' house. Graci also helped clear Pinky's street after Hurricane María. It's been a year since the hurricane, but Pinky still hears the shrieking of the wind in her nightmares.

"I'm going to volunteer at the coliseum packing emergency supplies. The mayor of San Juan, Mr. Rosso, is supposed to be there," Pinky says.

"Yikes, you have fun with that."

"What?"

"I don't know, I just get horrible vibes from that dude. He looks fake and there's that rumor about him cheating on his wife. Yay you for volunteering, though. I was calling to see if you wanted to help us clear streets, but it looks like you already have your philanthropy planned for the day."

"He can't be that bad. I don't subscribe to rumors. Thanks for the invite, maybe next time."

The local coliseum has turned into a city of skyscraper boxes and emergency supplies meant to aid those affected by the hurricane. Pinky smiled as she takes it all in. She weaves her way through make-shift walkways trying not to step on the children engaged in a very intense game of cops and robbers. The robbers use the boxes as cover when the boys in blue shoot and ask them to freeze.

"*Pillo! Pillo!*" the cops yell.

"*A mi no me cogen!*" one of the robbers says, sticking his tongue out.

He takes off and disappears behind some more boxes a few feet away. The cops pursue. Pinky follows the children with her gaze until the last kid cop vanishes behind a gaggle of annoyed teenage girls.

"*Si, buenas. ¿Cómo le ayudo?*"

Pinky jumps and turns, gripping her chest. A stranger stands behind Pinky expectantly.

"*Ay, disculpa*, sorry, I didn't hear you."

"Are you here to volunteer? If so, we need you back here. Not enough people, lots to do."

Before Pinky can respond, the stranger takes off. Pinky hurries along, making sure not to lose him in the crowd and risk annoying him any further. They arrive at a covered area with multiple, long rectangular folding tables covered in supplies from water and toilet paper to diapers and canned goods.

Fifteen minutes into packing boxes with the supplies, the sounds of children screeching, people talking and shouting above each other, music, and loudspeakers make Pinky's shoulders creep up to her ears. She tries to block it out by falling into a nice rhythm, water, paper towels, canned goods. Water, paper towels, canned goods. Water, paper towels, canned goods. Her shoulders eventually relax, and she finds a nice groove until a stranger demands her attention.

"*Hola*, I'm Daniel." He extends a hand toward Pinky.

She accepts. "Pinky."

"*Mucho gusto.*" He smiles as he shakes her hand. "Have you had a break yet?"

Pinky looks at her phone and realizes she's been working for four hours. She's parched and needs a bathroom break. Daniel leads Pinky to the nearest water cooler.

"How dare you take a break when people are dying?"

Pinky practically spits up the small amount of water she had managed to get in her mouth. She whips around to find Mr. Rosso, the mayor of San Juan, staring at her. Pinky's heart accelerates upon realizing the source of the critique. Pinky was eager to meet Mr. Rosso ever since he publicly supported same-sex marriage. This is a man of substance, Pinky had thought.

"We've been working for four hours, we just need some water," Daniel says.

"Some people have no water." Mr. Rosso looks them up

and down, grimaces, and walks off.

Pinky's eyes are wide, the cone still in her hand as she watches the mayor disappear into the crowd. He seems much shorter in person.

When Pinky and Daniel go back to work, the group of children that had been playing cops and robbers has settled down and turned their attention to drawing intricate patterns and designs on the already-packed boxes. A little girl draws a simple palm tree on a small piece of land that disappears into the ocean. A sun is setting behind the palm tree and ocean. It is not very detailed, but it makes Pinky smile.

At the end of the shift, Pinky rounds up her things. While checking her workstation, she notices Daniel in a heated discussion with someone wearing a badge, surely an employee. Daniel waves his hands around emphatically gesturing at the dozens of boxes crowding their workstation while the employee stands, leaning into one hip, an apathetic look on his face. After a bit more of the this, the employee shakes his head, says something, and walks away. Daniel flips off the unaware employee. Pinky makes her way to him.

"What was that about?"

"Ugh. It's nothing. We better move some of these boxes and make some room for tomorrow."

"Aren't they supposed to take these at the end of the day for distribution?"

"Supposed to."

Pinky arrives the next week bright and early. Her first week had been less than satisfactory, but her second will be great. She already knows the deal, so there won't be nearly as much awkwardness, and Mr. Rosso probably won't be there. He has not shown up since that first day. Plus, Pinky's good friend Robertito will be there to support both her and the cause. Robertito always tips big at Pinky's drag shows and boasts an avid social media following of more than fifteen thousand.

"*Gracias* for coming with me," Pinky says.

"*De nada, amor.* You know I'm always down." Robertito winks at her. "*Además*, you know what's up with my hometown, wrecked. Anything I can do for anyone, I'm in."

As they stroll into the coliseum, they immediately spot

Mr. Rosso. Pinky rolls her eyes. Of course, he's back today.

"What was that about?"

"What?"

"You got beef with Rosso?"

"He's terrible, totally rude."

Robertito squints. "*¿Qué pasó?* What happened?"

"*Mira*, here are some of our fabulous volunteers now." They are interrupted by Mr. Rosso who is approaching with a hoard of journalists and photographers.

Pinky's face scrunches up as she looks at the mayor. He extends a hand toward Robertito not bothering to make eye contact with Pinky.

"It's an honor to have you with us. This is a fine example of pure Puerto Rican spirit and pride." Mr. Rosso forces his hand into Robertito's.

His arm flails helplessly as Mr. Rosso forces his hand up and down, up and down. Robertito smiles awkwardly.

The photographers snap photo after photo. Journalists yell above each other trying to get Mr. Rosso's attention. Pinky watches, as he flashes a debonair smile. Robertito moves to pull his hand away, but Mr. Rosso grips his hand in place extending the shake.

"¡*Alcalde*! ¡*Alcalde*!"

Responding, Mr.Rosso tries to face as many cameras as possible.

"What's your name again?" he asks Robertito without breaking eye contact with the cameras.

They arrive at their designated work area. Only two of the ten people that had started volunteering last week remained, the rest are new. There are tons of packed boxes, more than when Pinky had left the week before.

"*Qué carajo?* What the hell?" Pinky's eyes fix on a familiar box with a drawing of a palm tree sitting on an island with a setting sun in the background.

"What?"

"Those boxes were supposed to go out days ago. I packed them last week."

"Are you sure?"

"Yes."

Pinky tries not to think about it and gets into her established packing routine, water, paper towels, canned goods.

"*Con permiso*, would you like some water?" Mr. Rosso extends a bottle of water toward Robertito. It drips with condensation.

Robertito slowly grabs the water bottle. "Gracias—"

"There are twelve other people here." Pinky gestures at the other volunteers.

Mr. Rosso's smile breaks for half a second, not long enough for any of the cameras to capture it. He momentarily glares at Pinky and turns to look at a young woman with a clipboard and disheveled hair. The young woman jerks into action signaling to some people behind her. Water bottles begin making their way to the volunteers.

When they offer Pinky a bottle, she takes it making a point to look Mr. Rosso in the eyes.

"Wow, thank you so much, you're so generous. How lucky we are to have such a magnanimous mayor." Pinky exaggerates a bow.

Mr. Rosso's façade doesn't break despite Pinky's provocation. He forces a smile and walks off, the hoard of journalists in tow.

Once Pinky and Robertito are done packing boxes for the day, they make their way out of the coliseum where there are trucks waiting to be filled. Pinky did not see a single truck last week. Mr. Rosso is standing in front of the closest truck saying something into the cameras about how the people of Puerto Rico are in dire need, which is why he will not rest until all of the emergency supplies have been successfully sent out. The jumpy and disheveled young woman from before stands behind Mr. Rosso barking orders at people to get the boxes ready for the mayor to load into the truck.

Pinky watches as the disheveled woman hands the box featuring the island sunset to Mr. Rosso. He snatches it out of her hands and grins. Pinky squints her eyes and furrows her brow as she stares at the mayor. The photographers eagerly snap photos as Mr. Rosso loads box after box onto the truck. He makes a big scene of it, moving slowly and deliberately ensuring there is ample time for everyone to capture the Kodak moment.

When Mr. Rosso notices Robertito in the crowd, he beckons

him close. Everyone turns in Robertito's direction. Robertito forces a smile and walks to Mr. Rosso. He places a hand on his shoulder and uses the other to lock Robertito in a handshake.

"Thank you again to the young people like this young man who are going out of their way to helps those in need."

The cameras desist finally, and Mr. Rosso stalks off without a word. The disheveled woman approaches Robertito.

"*Tienes* Instagram, *verdad*? What's your Insta handle?" she doesn't make eye contact with him.

Robertito responds, and the woman jots down the information, he turns and leaves.

"You're welcome," Robertito says to her back.

Robertito turns to face Pinky. "Can you believe this? Ridiculous."

Pinky's face grows hot. That man is faker than Pinky's Gucci bag and he has the nerve to scold others for drinking water.

"Wait, mister mayor!" Pinky runs after Mr. Rosso.

Mr. Rosso stops and turns. When he sees Pinky, the mayor's face tightens but he can't afford to ignore Pinky now that she has captured the attention of the hoard of journalists.

"I just want to say how impressed I am with how well this is organized. I mean, I packed those boxes you loaded last week, and they are already being shipped out. Such expediency." Pinky slow claps, her gaze still cutting through the mayor.

Mr. Rosso's eyes are wide but controlled, the reporters look at him expectantly.

"We are indeed well organized as these boxes were packed today." Mr. Rosso smiles at the crowd. "It's an easy mistake to make, the boxes look alike. People always think the worst of politicians. Not that I blame them. Bunch of crooks, am I right?" He aggressively elbows the disheveled woman who immediately starts laughing exaggeratedly at the mayor's joke.

Mr. Rosso's cohorts and the reporters follow suit, appearing satisfied with his response.

Pinky browses social media for any sign of her and Robertito's interactions with Mr. Rosso the day before. It isn't long before she finds what she's looking for. The image of Mr. Rosso and Robertito standing in front of the truck is featured on the Puerto Rico Recovers Instagram page. Mr. Rosso poses enthusiastically with a sheepish looking Robertito. Pinky shakes her head, her face turning slightly red. She picks up her phone and dials Graci.

"Hey Pink, what's the stink?"

"Nothing, baby. Are you going to be clearing streets today?"

"You know it. We are meeting up at the location for Loverbar. Why? You want to come?"

"Yeah, I'll meet you there. By the way, you going to get that place going any time soon, because mama needs a place to perform. You know these gay clubs out here be transphobic as hell sometimes."

"I'm working on it, I promise. The hurricane set us back, but it didn't stop us. Is volunteering with Rosso not all it's cracked up to be?"

"Not at all. We should really do something about how terrible he is."

"It's not just him, the whole administration is a shit show."

"Then maybe we should do something about that."

Chapter Four

Gassed in Drag

Pinky and Valeria stumble down the cobblestone road, their four-inch-stilettos catching in the spaces between the aging bricks. Luckily, the jumble of people around them serve as a constant balance post. They are more like sardines than women in the overcrowded can that was Old San Juan that evening. Pinky is used to wigs and heat, but this is other-worldly.

Her black wig creates more sweat than usual, but the look is worth it. Usually, she'd be sporting the wig and stilettos in an air-conditioned club for a badass performance laced with intense yet subtle sociopolitical commentary. But now, she is bringing the act to the streets because, well, honestly, there is no other choice, not for Pinky. A year ago, Pinky found out how negligent Puerto Rican politicians were during hurricane relief. Now, she finds out the governor, J. Navarro, is not just corrupt but also a total dick. The homophobic comments were all Pinky needed to join the coup against him. The fact that he mocked the deaths resulting from the hurricane, accused all women of being whores, and admitted to corrupt behavior only fueled her fire.

Pinky decides to attend the protest against the governor in drag despite the potential harassment that inevitably comes with going out in drag on a heavily hetero island. She's proud of her look, ruby red lipstick, a black T-shirt that portrays *una sola Estrella*, and a sign that proclaims—Always a whore, never a thief. The crowd is agreeable enough as Pinky and Valeria make their way to the front of the protest, no pushing, no shoving.

"¡*Siempre puta, nunca pilla*! ¡*Siempre puta, nunca pilla*!" Pinky and Valeria chant, their heads held high as they march.

Valeria waves enthusiastically at someone a few feet away in the crowd. Pinky follows her line of sight and spots Robertito. She hasn't seen him since they volunteered at the coliseum together. Pinky waves at Robertito who smiles and waves back. The people playing instruments and chanting create a high and cohesive energy. *Panderos* and cowbells help keep the beat while guiros and sticks grind and strike. Pinky forgets about the uneven footing and begins flowing with the music. The groove is disrupted by someone bumping into her.

"*¡Qué perra!*" A drunk woman snaps her fingers at Pinky, as she fumbles to take a picture with her phone.

Pinky smiles, poses for the picture, and gives a half-hearted fist pump.

"I knew that look would kill," Valeria says, looking at Pinky's fan.

"I don't think she gets it. She's just excited to see a drag queen."

"The sign makes it pretty clear, no?"

"She didn't care about the message. She's probably that girl that climbs on stages during drag shows."

Valeria laughs. "Ay, Pinky. Didn't that happen to you last year?"

"Yes. I almost cut a bitch." Pinky can't help but smirk at the memory.

Valeria grabs Pinky by the arm and they continue chanting, putting the drunk fan behind them. They get to the front of the protest where the barricade is with the people on one side and the police on the other. The *policía* of Puerto Rico stand statuesque in their riot gear, as the people chant on with fury and musical instruments. A few empty water bottles and straws flutter over the barricade and onto the cops. The cops ignore the first few but get more and more jittery as trash continues to fly.

"*¡Siempre puta, nunca pilla! ¡NAVARRO RENUNCIA, ahora no orita!* Resign, Navarro, now not later," Pinky and Valeria chant.

The people around them join in.

"*¡Siempre puta, nunca pilla! NAVARRO RENUNCIA, ahora no orita! ¡Siempre puta, nunca pilla! ¡NAVARRO RENUNCIA, ahora no orita!*"

Goosebumps rise on Pinky's sweaty skin as she notices the small, but powerful following they accrued. A smile stretches across her face unconsciously, but it's quickly erased by a shove that hurls her forward a few inches.

"*Mami, estás bien?*" Valeria asks, grabbing hold of Pinky's arm.

Pinky shrugs it off. "Yeah, I'm fine."

Pinky and Valeria continue to chant.

"¡*Siempre puta, nunca pilla*! ¡*NAVARRO RENUNCIA, ahora no orita*! ¡*Siempre puta, nunca pilla*! ¡*NAVARRO RENUNCIA, ahora no orita*!"

Another shove sends both Pinky and Valeria forward, forcing them into the barricade separating them from la *policía*. The policemen directly in front of them flinch. Then, all the policemen lined up behind the barricade tense up.

Pinky catches herself on one of the orange dividers. Valeria does too, but not quite as successfully, her forearm caught the edge of the orange divider forcefully, it will certainly leave a bruise.

"Okay," Valeria says. "You need to take your heels off because this is about to get real."

Pinky takes notice of the cops starting to change their stances from neutral to combat-ready. She removes her heels and slips on the sneakers she has tucked away in her backpack. The moment she shoves her heels into the bag, the crowd crashes into her like a wave on a desperate surfer. Before she knows what's happening, someone, she assumes Valeria, grabs her arm, and pulls her out of the onslaught and into the mass of panicked people rushing from the expanding cloud of tear gas. It's not long before the tear gas reaches them. The fog makes it impossible to keep sight of Valeria. Pinky struggles to hold onto Valeria's hand as the crowd pushes and pulls threatening to break her grip. That grip is all keeping her and Valeria together. If she loses the grip on her hand—Fuck.

Pinky is lost in a yellow limbo, stumbling downhill, trying not to fall on the cobblestone. The loss of sight, the screaming, and the constant physical battery in addition to the panic and fear of being alone and in danger have her operating on instinct.

"Valeria. Valeria!" Pinky cries though she does not know why. How can anyone hear her in this madness?

Once Pinky runs far enough for the gas to clear a bit, she finds a corner to safely stand. She unsuccessfully searches her bag for her phone. Crap, it must be in Valeria's bag. She scans the crowd. With any luck she will find Valeria or someone she knows. There's safety in numbers. But there is no sign of Valeria, not that Pinky could distinguish much within the speeding throng. She catches a glimpse of Robertito as he rushes by caught in the current of chaos.

"Robertito," Pinky shouts after him.

The back of Robertito's head, which is all Pinky can see, continues rushing forward. He does not turn.

"Robertito!" She tries to be louder, to catch up to him, but the crowd is too compressed.

A gap appears and Robertito's entire body comes into view. Pinky dives for the opening, but it closes before she can make it through. The bodies blocking her way are solid and send her crashing to the ground amid a stampede of anonymous feet. Her knees and palms throb. She tries to stand but is knocked by a passing body. She tries to stand again but is caught in the face by a knee. Pinky falls to the ground, a high-pitched ring in her ears. Her hands find her head and hold tight as she shifts her body into a fetal position.

After a few seconds, her body starts going numb. A hand finds her arm, takes hold, and yanks. The mystery hero pulling her through the crowd slowly materializes as they run. Robertito. Once the crowd thins, Pinky jumps into his arms. Initially, he is taken aback but quickly returns the hug. They stand in that corner for about an hour until they start finding people they know. There is still no sign of Valeria, but at least Pinky is not alone.

Robertito and Pinky don't exchange words beyond the initial murmurings of concern. Robertito observes Pinky's bruised body, her legs already becoming a collage of black and blue. Pinky tries to wave off his concern, but he continues looking at her like a wounded kitten.

When Valeria finally surfaces, Pinky practically tackles her. Valeria pulls something out of her purse which she had somehow managed to hold on to during the chaos. She offers Pinky her phone.

"Please keep your phone in your bag." Valeria smiles at

Pinky.

Pinky notices that Valeria also had quite the experience. Her hair is a disheveled mess, her mascara and eyeliner have run, her knees are scraped, and she has the beginnings of a shiner appearing on her face.

Getting out of Old San Juan takes forever. Pinky, Valeria, Robertito, and two others pile into Valeria's car. They sit in the car for two hours before getting out of the city. They do not speak much while they sit in stand-still traffic. Pinky sits in the back behind the driver's seat her head resting on the window. She doesn't normally allow her forehead to contact people's car window's, not only did it smudge their window, but it smudged her makeup, but today, she doesn't give a fuck. The colorful buildings preserving the colonial aesthetic of Old San Juan whiz by in a haze as the crew tries to decide on a place to decompress. If Loverbar was open, it would be the perfect spot, but Graci will get it going soon enough.

They finally decide on Pinky's place since it's the closest. There aren't enough leftovers to feed everyone, but Pinky will figure something out, she has some pasta she can make do with. Pinky gets to work in the kitchen while Valeria, who knows her kitchen well from many a drunken sleepover, serves up some drinks for everyone. Pinky hasn't had time to re-up on booze either, so the drinks are a strange combination of whatever booze with orange juice.

When drinks start flowing, people start relaxing and chatting about what transpired.

"Oh my god, *nena*, yes, I fell too. Got my ass trampled, can't you tell?" Valeria points at her knees and face.

Everyone laughs approvingly. Gotta love the magic of booze.

"I had to literally pull this one up from the ground," Robertito gestures toward Pinky.

"*Mira, cállate!*" Pinky smacks Robertito on the shoulder.

He takes it with a smile.

The evening carries on with everyone telling their individual stories of terror and resilience. Robertito saw someone get knocked unconscious. Valeria, besides being banged up, had helped a horrified eighteen-year-old find their group, and that's why it took so long for her to find Pinky. The others at the table have similar stories. Mariela got separated from her partner and had not managed to find her. Jorge got tear-gassed the worst. He wasn't far from where the cop tossed the first canister.

They indulge in a bit of ganja to facilitate sharing the barrage of thoughts and frustrations that remained. Pinky looks at her bruised legs and observes the other battered faces taking a huge hit of the blunt being passed around. She exhales, releasing a cloud of smoke and sinks into her chair. Her muscles and mind melt as she passes the blunt.

"I don't know if I'll go to another protest." Valeria takes a hit.

"Well, on the plus side, the drag ball is coming up," Robertito says placing a hand on Valeria's shoulder. "It shouldn't be as bad as this."

Valeria looks at Robertito expectantly.

"What drag ball?"

"Seriously, I found out before you?"

Valeria rolls her eyes. "Just spill, please."

"There's a *cuir* group organizing a drag ball in protest of the governor. I think your friend Graci is involved. You should ask her about it."

Robertito, Valeria, and the others immediately start talking above each other theorizing how badass the drag ball will be. Pinky is silent still laying back in her chair.

"Pinky, Valeria stares at Pinky. "Do you want to go?"

Pinky sits up, rubs her neck, and sighs.

"Fuck it, I'm in."

Chapter Five

Private Property

I hate the roads in Puerto Rico. The number of potholes and shoddy patch jobs make any drive a turbulent nightmare. My boyfriend Eduardo's driving makes the ride more treacherous. He's going fifteen miles above the speed limit and hitting potholes like it ain't no thang.

"Oh my God, slow down. You're going to murder my car."

I shouldn't have let him drive, but he insisted. My boyfriend cares an awful lot about taking on the guy role in the relationship. I know he's only trying to be nice because he chose to go to that protest against Governor Navarro with that slut Mauro instead of coming to my niece's birthday party. It's not like he didn't know weeks in advance. Eduardo swears Mauro is just a friend, but I have my doubts. Yesterday, the idiot came home trashed and reeking of beer hours after the protest was finished. He barely even looked at me when he arrived. He just went straight to the bathroom to shower.

I need to call Lola and make sure she's all set to go to her hair and make-up appointment. Her next drag show is tonight, and I must make sure she looks fierce. I dial Lola's number.

"*Hola,* baby. I just want to double check that you have a ride to your make-up and hair appointment. Good, it took me forever to get you in with Marcel. Make sure you have the inspiration pictures for him."

I can feel Eduardo's judgmental gaze burning a hole through me. If he cares that much about having my attention, he shouldn't have bailed on me yesterday.

"Lola, don't be late. He's overbooked, you'll lose your appointment, okay?"

I swear, it's like having two partners. At least Lola appreciates having me around. Helping her with her drag performances is the only kind of work I actually enjoy.

"Okay, I'll be at the venue at eight sharp. Don't be late."

I hang up the phone and look at Eduardo.

"What?"

"You're still helping that mess?"

"She's not a mess, and yes. I want to be an event planner, remember? This is legitimate experience."

"Right, legitimate."

"It's better than just wasting my time as a waiter."

"It's not wasting time if you plan on managing or even opening your own restaurant."

I don't respond. Instead, I look out the window and watch the trees whizz by. He never misses an opportunity to bash my dreams. Does he even care about my happiness?

"Are we almost there?" I ask, hoping to change the subject.

"Yes. We'll need to do a bit of hiking once we get there."

"Ugh." I hate hiking. "Why couldn't we just go to Ocean Park? It's closer to home and doesn't involve hiking."

"I told you, this beach is special. I've been going there for years. Don't you want a special day?"

No, you want a special day because you feel guilty about ditching me yesterday. I should say that out loud. Come on, Xavi, just say it—but, let's face it, I'm not going to. I don't want to start another argument.

After ten minutes of silence in the car, Eduardo finally takes an exit. Two stoplights and a left and a right later, we arrive at an isolated road with vegetation threatening to overtake the asphalt. He parks on the side of the road.

"Here."

I look around and notice a construction site nestled in the brush a few feet down the road.

"Are you sure we're allowed to be here?"

"Once we're on the beach, it shouldn't be a problem. It's getting there that's tricky."

"So, no."

"I've been coming here for years, and it's never been a problem."

I point at the house being constructed a few feet away. "There's construction now. Someone will be pissed we're walking through here."

Eduardo rolls his eyes. He's doing that a lot more often.

"You worry too much."

"No, I don't."

Eduardo turns to face me, a direct challenge. I drop my gaze and focus on digging through my fanny pack for that sweet, sweet ganja. I can't wait until it's recreationally legal. I find the joint I rolled earlier and spark it up. Inhale, hold, exhale. As the smoke slips through my parted lips, my muscles soften.

"*Quieres*? Do you want a hit?" I offer Eduardo.

He shakes his head. "I'll wait until we get to the beach."

Suit yourself. I take one more hit and place the rest of the joint in my fanny pack with the rest of the green. With our backpacks in tow, Eduardo leads us through an opening in the vegetation and onto a path made by years of trudging feet. As we walk, the heat and humidity create pit stains the size of hefty pancakes underneath my arms. I can feel droplets of sweat forming on my forehead and back. I'm definitely going to break out after today.

We walk for about five minutes in silence. Despite the marked path, dried palms, grass, coconuts, roots, and uneven sand make the trek difficult. Good thing we didn't bring a big cooler. I swat my legs to stop the itch, this is bug paradise.

Why couldn't we just go to a beach that has easier access? I'm not trying to get the police called on me by whomever bought this property. I wonder whose it is. Probably someone off the island. I don't know any Puerto Ricans that are buying, much less constructing property these days. Not that my sample size is so large, but when all you hear in the news are complaints about the economy and then see wealthy outsiders moving down here to work in pharmaceutical companies or government agencies you begin to wonder.

We walk by a sign that lets people know it's private property— *Propiedad Privada – Prohibido Traspasar* .

"That sign makes me sick." Eduardo scrunches his nose as he looks at the sign. "That's why yesterday's protest was so important. That's why getting Navarro out of office is so important."

It's not that I don't agree, it's that I think Eduardo is a poser, and it bugs the hell out of me that he uses the protests against the governor as an excuse to party. Not that he'll ever

admit that. It didn't matter that my mother was excited to see
him because he never comes around. Eduardo says it was
important that he show up and demonstrate his support for the
cause. Navarro is a rat, and he needs to pay for stealing and
insulting our people.

"How much farther?" I ask trying to distract myself from
my negative self-talk.

My friend Graci insists that our self-talk is the greatest
manifesting force in our lives. What you think, you attract.

"Ten maybe fifteen minutes. Tired already? You should
really start coming to the gym."

"I'm not tired, I was just curious." We continue in silence
for a few seconds.

This has been the new normal. Small but hurtful comments, little pebbles of condescension hurled at me on the
reg. If I say anything, I'm too sensitive or inconsiderate of
the way he is. As Eduardo says, he's just honest, not mean.

It wasn't always like this. We used to be freaking adorable, the couple everyone loved to hate. I didn't believe the
friends that told me it was just the honeymoon phase. For our
first Valentine's Day together in twenty fifteen, he came
home from work early, decorated the apartment with flower
petals and candles, and cooked us up a steak dinner, fancy
bottle of red wine included. As for dessert, well, we were
each other's dessert. No one had ever done anything like that
for me. I knew then Eduardo was it, the prince of my pretty
boy dreams, and no amount of time together would change
the love and consideration he dished up daily. Or so I
thought. Fast-forward four years. Valentine's Day twenty
nineteen, he wasn't even home. I don't know what happened.
Had he grown bored with me? Was I no longer attractive?

The eye-rolling and huffing and puffing had already
begun by the time Hurricane María hit in twenty seventeen. I
guess that's how long our honeymoon phase was, two years.
The hurricane didn't help our already deteriorating relationship. It destroyed the island and our patience. No one could
get anywhere because the roads were blocked with debris, so
people spent a lot of time at home. There was no power or
running water for weeks and business came to a halt. Both of
the restaurants where Eduardo and I worked shut down.

Getting gas was a nightmare. Once, we waited three hours to fill up our car. Getting groceries had to be a planned affair, and when we made it to the store, all the essentials like rice, beans, bread, and coffee were scarce. Hungry and bored was not a great combination. Without the Internet to distract us, every little annoyance and pet peeve became magnified. But I didn't mind him as much as he seemed to mind me. That much became clear the day he yelled at me for sneezing and snorting too loudly. He used to say my sneezes were cute. I can't help that I have terrible allergies. I tried to be kind and understanding like my mother recommended. It's too bad Eduardo didn't receive the same piece of advice.

"What's wrong?"

Eduardo is looking back at me through scrunched eyes. I must have what he calls the look on my face. He knows something is on my mind.

"Oh, nothing. Just thinking." I bring my attention back to the hike.

Roots and fallen trees still obstruct the path, but I'm getting used to it.

"Still nervous we'll get caught?"

This time it's me who rolls my eyes. "Ay, come on. I'm just kidding." Eduardo tries to take my hand, but I pull it away.

"Xavi, *no es por nada*, but I'm trying here."

He must be joking.

"You call making verbal jabs at me all morning trying? You've been a jerk this whole time. I don't even know why we bothered with this stupid beach day."

My heart is pounding, but it feels good to tell him off. Now the inevitable fallout. Here it comes.

"You're right, I'm sorry. I'm just tired from the protest yesterday."

Hold up, he's apologizing now? This is new. Why is he apologizing?

"Makes sense. You and Mauro stayed out pretty late." I'm aware of my tone and hope he is, too.

I pick up my pace and walk past him making sure to bump his shoulder on the way.

"We all did, it wasn't just us. I told you that. Plus, we

weren't partying."

"Yes you—ow!"

I feel a sharp pain in my leg and look down to find its source is a sharp stick hidden in a pile of dead leaves. I was too busy being angry to notice it as I brushed past Eduardo. Blood oozes from the gash on my leg.

"*Sea la madre*, damn it."

"Let me see." Eduardo reaches for my leg.

"I'm fine." I slap his hand away.

"Xavi, I'm trying to help. Just let me clean it up."

The blood slithers down my leg. It makes my head spin. I hate blood.

"Fine." I plop down on a rock and succumb to his request.

Eduardo gets a first aid kit out of his backpack. I used to make fun of him for carrying that. Not seriously, like flirtatious mockery. When we first started dating, I called him my sexy boy scout. I loved his preparedness.

Eduardo softly runs an alcohol swab over the wound, parting the blood like the red sea. I suck my teeth at the sting, and goosebumps emerge on my arm. Despite the pain, it feels nice. It's been a while since I felt him caress me. I guess it takes getting physically injured for him to touch me these days.

"Ya, all better." Eduardo kisses the gash.

My cheeks grow hot, and I look away. I don't want him to see how quickly my anger dissipated.

"Are you blushing?" Eduardo laughs.

"Don't make fun of me."

"I'm not, I'm not. It's cute."

My heart beats like the timbal drum Eduardo plays at Christmas parties. He's so good at beating those drums.

"Thanks for cleaning my cut." I should at least be grateful.

"*De nada*." Eduardo takes hold of my face and kisses me, slow.

My whole body is on fire. Damn him and his delicious lips. Maybe I'm overreacting. Maybe it's me whose been a dick. Is it possible I've been projecting? I have been under tons of stress since I went back to school for event management.

Eduardo didn't think it was a good idea.

"Now, let's get to that beach." Eduardo walks off.

He looks back at me and winks. I smile and follow.

The brush clears as we get closer to the beach, and walking gets easier. There's still roots and ruffage, but it no longer blankets the ground. The sand is smooth and the air thick with salt and humidity. Luckily, the palm trees provide adequate coverage. Occasionally, when the wind blows, the sun peeks through the palms showering us in a drizzle of warm light. I guess hiking is kind of nice.

"Why don't we get some music going and get the party started. You have the speaker, right?" Eduardo asks.

"*Si*," I respond, stopping to retrieve it from my bag.

I connect my phone to the speaker, but it dies instantly.

"*Mierda*, I'm out of battery."

"That's what you get for gossiping with Lola on the phone the entire way here."

"You're exaggerating, and I was not gossiping. I told you, I'm helping Lola with her next show. She wants me to be her manager."

"You could be managing that new restaurant where you work in no time if you gave up that drag show foolishness."

Not this again. Deep breath, deep breath. Back to the music.

"Hand me your phone, I'll connect it to the speaker." I extend my hand and wait.

Eduardo reaches for his phone but stops.

"Oh, on second thought, why don't we just enjoy the natural sounds. It's like that ambient shit you love but real life, and what's more relaxing than that?"

Eduardo takes exaggerated deep breaths while doing prayer hands.

"Okay, but I'll need music once we get to the beach."

"Deal."

"Hey, what are you two doing?"

We both whip around. A middle-aged man in a suit is yelling at us from a distance. I knew we'd get in trouble.

"Come on, let's just go back," I urge Eduardo.

"No way. These jerks come here and think they own the place. Well, they don't own the beach, and we deserve to be on it if we want."

"This is private property, pro-prie-dad pri-va-da." The man takes his time enunciating in his best Puerto Rican accent.

"We're not bothering anyone. We just want to get to the beach."

"No, no, no. You can't walk through here." The man starts walking toward us. "I'll call the police if you don't leave. You're trespassing, tras-pa-san-do."

Eduardo turns to look at me. "Get ready to run."

"Run?"

"Go!"

Eduardo takes off. "Come on!"

The man is still advancing. "Hey, stop. *Propiedad privada.*"

I take off after Eduardo. He runs through the woods like a gay Puerto Rican Tarzan jumping over logs, dodging roots and rocks. I try my best to keep up without falling, I'm not nearly as graceful. We start losing the man quickly. He can't run in that suit, and boy is my lazy ass grateful. Maybe I should start hitting the gym.

"Can you slow down? I think we lost him," I say, breathing hard.

 Eduardo slows down.

"You all right?"

I nod my head.

"Well, the good news is, we're almost there."

"You don't think he'll be able to find us?"

"I don't think he'll bother."

"Okay, carry on, Tarzan. But I need a drink first."

Eduardo chuckles, I'm not sure if he's annoyed or amused. He puts his bag down and removes a thermos. He offers it to me. I accept and take a generous swig. A gust of wind blows through the palm trees with enough force to rattle some coconuts. I imagine one of the coconuts falling and hitting me on the head. It's been one of my greatest fears ever since I saw a sign on the beach as a kid. "Caution. Beware of falling coconuts." When I asked my older brother what would happen if a coconut fell on my head, he simply told me I would die.

"Are you done with the thermos? Once we pass these fallen trees, we just need to climb some rocks and boom, we're there."

Five palm trees lay on the ground. A footprint of Hurricane María no doubt. We hopped over the trunks. Jumping over the fifth one, Eduardo's phone falls out of his pocket. He doesn't notice. I pick it up and go to call out to him but stop when I see a message from Mauro on the screen. I look at Eduardo to make sure he hasn't noticed, and I punch in the security code he doesn't know that I know. I didn't mean to memorize it, I swear. It's only four digits, and he unlocks his phone in front of me all the time.

"Yesterday was awesome. We should definitely go to the next protest," Mauro had written.

That seems innocent enough. I press forward after Eduardo.

"Hey, Edu. You dropped your—"

His phone vibrates in my hand. It's Mauro again.

"Or maybe we can just skip the protest and get straight to the afterparty. I love that thing you do with your tongue."

My vision is blurred by tears, and I'm overcome by a wave of nausea.

"What?" Eduardo turns.

I stand frozen with his phone in my hand. Eduardo feels his pockets then looks back up at me, eyes wide. He briskly walks to me, takes his phone, and stuffs it in his pocket.

"Why are you looking through my phone?"

I open my mouth to speak, but nothing comes out.

"Did you read my messages?"

I should yell, scream, call him what he is, a filthy cheater, but instead, I turn around and take off running. I can barely see anything because of the waterworks, but I don't care. Somehow, I'm able to sprint through the vegetation without falling. I can't even feel the gash on my leg. My only goal is to get as far away from Eduardo as possible. The car. I just need to get to the car. Luckily, I have the keys. If there's one thing I'm grateful to Eduardo for, it's insisting that we take my car.

I crash into something and knock it to the ground. Wiping my eyes, I see the man that had been yelling at us to get off his *propiedad*. He has two officers in tow, both of whom just stare at me with wide eyes. I quicky shove my way through them and continue running. Will they come after me?

"There are two of them. The other one must be up ahead," the man says from the ground.

"Should we go after that one?"

Crap, they are going to come after me. Catch me if you can, sucker.

"Come back here!" one of the cops yells.

I pick up the pace running as fast as I've ever run. I'm Tarzan now, weaving through trees and dodging branches. A gust of wind blows, and it feels as though it's pushing me along. I still hear the cop chasing me, but I don't stop. I don't even look back. My chest heaves as I pant and run, pant and run.

Has it been five minutes or fifteen? I no longer hear anyone chasing me, but I'm not taking any chances. I keep running until I pass both the *Propiedad Privada* sign and the house under construction. The clearing that leads to the car is up ahead. I stumble out of the brush and onto the road where the car is parked. Breathing hard, I search through my fanny pack for the keys. I feel the cold metal on my fingers. Score. I shove the keys into the driver door, yank the door open, get in, slam it shut, and start the car.

I hit the gas, take off, and drive out of the isolated street. First a left, then a right. Perfect, here's the first stoplight. I think I made it. The stoplight is red, so I wait, grateful for a moment to breathe and calm down. You're okay, Xavi. You're okay.

A cop car pulls up next to me. Crap, crap. My heart races. Did they call for back up? No, no way. I'm just paranoid. Act natural. Keeping my gaze locked on the red light, I try to steady my breathing. I feel the cop in the passenger seat turn to look at me. I don't move. Come on, turn green. Turn green. The light turns green, and I wait, hoping the cop car will go before me indicating I'm of no interest to them. After a second, the cop car advances and turns left. I sigh deeply, slumping my body into the seat. Thank gay god.

Once I'm on the highway and certain I'm good, the guilt settles in. What if Eduardo gets arrested? Sure, he cheated, but does he deserve to go to jail for it? Maybe I should call him. The message from Mauro flashes in my head.

I love that thing you do with your tongue.

Screw it, Eduardo can find his own way home.

Chapter Six

Staying Alive

"*Por favor*, let's go. It's not going to be like the last protest." Valeria drops to her knees and grabs hold of Sammy's legs.

Sammy is busy texting his father who wants to make sure Sammy will be at his grandmother's birthday party. Of course, Sammy will go, but he won't like it. Sammy's father says she tries her best but the constant deadnaming and misgendering always leaves Sammy feeling deflated and empty.

Valeria forces Sammy to look at the promo on Instagram.

La Renuncia Ball, July 17, 2019 / Plaza de Armas – Haus of Resistance.

Sammy shakes his head. Valeria is either ridiculously hopeful or ready to get trampled and harassed. This is the Haus of Resistance's first performance, and the police will surely be on deck to break up the *patería*, the gayness. If there's something authority hates, it's a bunch of queers, prancing around demanding justice.

"How do you know it won't go to shit?" Sammy says, still looking at the promo. "That protest you went to with Pinky ended up in a mess of tear gas."

"Think of this more as—an artistic exhibition than a protest. Plus, there probably won't be as many people."

"Did you forget what happened to Vanesa? That was only a few months ago."

Sammy shakes at the thought of the transgender woman lying on the floor, her face barely recognizable from the beating she took. She survived, physically, but hasn't been out of her apartment since. Sammy and Valeria know her from the drag scene. Apparently, some guy took offense to the fact he fell for that pervert's act. Sammy wonders if Vanesa's grandmother misses her.

"That's exactly why we have to do this." Valeria takes Sammy's hand.

Maybe it won't get violent this time, or maybe it will

be worse.

Sammy receives a text from his father. "I have my grandmother's birthday that day. If I go, I'll have to meet you there."

Valeria sucks through her teeth. "Well, maybe family bonding won't be that bad."

Sammy scoffs.

"We'll see."

"¡*Ay, llegó mi estrella*! My star is here." Sammy's *Abuelita* frantically waves her arms at Sammy urging him to join her.

Sammy smiles and waves as he makes his way to them. His *Abuelita* sits in her favorite chair which she makes her son move wherever she goes. It was her late husband's chair and she refused to sit anywhere else since he died. Sammy's *Abuelita* is surrounded by uncles, aunts, and cousins, only about half of whom he recognizes. With ten aunts and uncles on his father's side, it's difficult to keep track.

"*Bendición, Abuelita.*" Sammy kneels by his grandmother, requesting the traditional blessing and kiss that all Puerto Ricans request of their family elders upon greeting.

"*Que Dios me la bendiga y la Virgen me la acompañe.* May God bless you and keep you."

Sammy winces at the misgendering but kisses his *Abuelita* on the cheek. His *Abuelita* pulls him in for a hug. Sammy is initially a bit stiff but soon relaxes and buries his face into her neck. Sammy inhales and smiles when the fresh scent hits his nostrils.

Sammy finds it endearing and amusing that his grandmother uses a popular baby water cologne-like perfume.

"*Gracias por venir*, thank you for coming." *Abuelita* lingers in the hug.

"*Claro, Abuelita,* of course." Sammy remains in the hug until his grandmother decides to end it.

When Sammy's parents were hustling trying to make enough to pay the bills, his grandparents looked after him. It was with *Abuelita* that he first saw *The Birdcage* at twelve years old. Little did his *Abuelita* know Sammy was fantasizing about the fabulous and colorful suits and ensembles Robin Williams and Nathan Lane wore in the film. After that,

Sammy took to sneaking into his Abuelito's closet whenever he had the chance. Decades of fashion hid in that deceivingly uninteresting closet. Sammy was particularly fond of his Abuelito's seventies silver platform boots and lime green bellbottoms. They were the opposite of Sammy's usual look of jeans and a graphic tee. He always wore a graphic tee featuring one of his many heroes, Joan Jett, David Bowie, Cher. All bad bitches.

Sammy had never felt more like himself than he did in those platforms and bellbottoms. He was pure John Travolta in *Saturday Night Fever*, living that seventies east coast disco dream. The man he always wanted to be, suave yet masculine, a lady's man that the people knew and loved.

The first day he dressed up was the day he dropped Samantha and embraced Samuel. He put the bellbottoms and boots on without looking in the mirror. The feel of the bright, polyester blend on his flesh made him smile. Although the boots fit a bit loosely, they elevated him an extra four inches. Sammy puffed out his chest and breathed deep before stepping in front of the mirror.

Sammy took in his reflection. He looked like his Abuelito in all those old photographs *Abuelita* forced all guests to peruse. The Bee Gee's "Stayin' Alive" played in his head as Sammy strutted around the room working the hustle moves he'd picked up from Travolta.

Sammy sang, extending his arms diagonally and pointing his fingers. Sammy took hold of the spot where he would someday have his glorious crotch and pumped his hips, thrusting like Travolta on the prowl in the disco tech.

"*¡Ay, Dios mío!* Oh, my God."

Sammy had not noticed that *Abuelita* had walked in and was watching his performance.

"*¡Quítate eso!* Take that off! What's wrong with you?" Her eyes were wide, as she took in the sight of her beloved granddaughter dressed like a boy and moving like a heathen.

"*No puedo.* I can't handle losing both my husband and granddaughter the same year. *Ay, Señor Jesus Cristo*, give me strength."

Sammy never dressed that flamboyantly again.

His *Abuelita* spends the next few minutes after greeting

Sammy bragging about how well he is doing at the university. He's a senior and about to graduate as an accountant. Sammy smiles and answers questions from family members.

"*Oye, y tienes novio?* Do you have a boyfriend?" Someone Sammy doesn't recognize asks, leaving him momentarily stunned.

Sammy laughs, looking around for a way out. "Who has time for that?" Sammy keeps laughing awkwardly. "I'm grabbing a drink, does anyone need anything, *Abuelita*?"

"*Ay, si, un cafecito, por favor.*"

Sammy smiles. "A coffee it is."

The celebration continues without incident for a while.

"Thank you for—you know, making sure *Abuelita* is happy on her day," Sammy's father tells him off to the side while *Abuelita* blows out her candles.

He places a hand on Sammy's shoulder and gently squeezes. Sammy places his hand on his father's and returns the squeeze.

"Sure, *Papi*, no problem. I love her and want her to be happy even if—"

"It's not her fault, she grew up differently."

Sammy chugs the rest of the white wine he's drinking.

"She loves you more than anything."

"I know." Sammy puts down the empty glass and gives his father a half-hearted smile. "I should go wish her a happy birthday."

"*Felicidades, Abuelita.* Happy Birthday."

"*Ay, mi niña preciosa*, my beautiful girl. *Qué mucho te quiero*, how I love you." Sammy's *Abuelita* slides the back of her fingers down Sammy's cheek. "You should really grow out your hair, though, you look like a boy."

A stabbing pain in his gut makes Sammy jerk. Sammy trembles as he stands. It's more difficult than expected, his legs feel weak like his knees could give out at any moment.

"I, uh, have to go to the bathroom." Sammy walks away, his brow furrowed.

Sammy avoids eye contact with everyone as he power-walks to his car. His father jogs behind him trying to catch up.

"Sammy, leaving already?"

"*Si*, Papi. I have that event, remember? It's important, and I'm late."

"Did you say goodbye to your grandmother? She loves having you here, and you know she hasn't been feeling too well lately."

Sammy shakes his head and takes a deep breath.

"*Ay*, Papi. Please don't guilt-trip me. Look at all of these people." Sammy gestures at the crowd of relatives circling and swarming both *Abuelita* and the buffet table.

"She won't miss me. Plus, I'll be back later this week. I promise. I have to go."

Sammy desperately needs a wardrobe change after going to his *Abuelita*'s. He decides on his Bowie tee and black jeans with classic Converse sneakers. He considers wearing last year's Halloween costume, which was an imitation of his grandfather's bellbottoms and platform boots but decides against it, afraid the outfit would land him an ass-whooping.

Old San Juan is packed as usual with tipsy tourists and lively locals looking for a good time. Sammy weaves his way expertly through the crowd his shoulders hunched and head down, a master of blending in. Sammy's phone vibrates in his pocket. It's a text from his father. Sammy shuts his eyes and takes a deep breath. Sammy prepares to open and read the message, but a blonde in stilettos, who's busy looking at her phone too, bumps into him sending his phone to the ground.

"Excuse you," the blonde says, still looking at her phone.

"*Si claro*, of course it was my fault," Sammy says under his breath, as he squats down to retrieve the phone.

It's cracked. Great. Sammy tries to open the message from his father, but the cracked screen makes it impossible. Oh, well.

When Sammy arrives at the Plaza de Armas where the drag ball is being held, he stops a minute to see if he can locate Valeria. The plaza is full. The crowd is a colorful menagerie of tourists, locals, and queers from across the spectrum. Music is blaring through speakers as people mingle and show off their protest best. Sammy thinks about how his *Abuelita* would react to the flamboyant outfits and provocative protest signs calling for the resignation of the governor.

"¡*Finalmente*! You made it. I low-key thought you were

going to bail." Valeria wraps her arms around Sammy lifting him off the ground.

Sammy gasps and kicks his feet.

"Claro, I said I'd be here. Now, put me down, *cabrona*!"

Valeria drops him. "Sorry, mi amor. I'm just so excited. Can you believe this crowd and this energy?" Valeria throws her arms into the air, closes her eyes, and begins to twirl. "Pure magic. So different from last time."

Valeria twirling makes Sammy smile. He feels his body loosen. He can talk to his father when he gets home. It'll be good to disconnect for a while.

"Look. Pinky is here." Valeria points to the middle of the plaza where Pinky is standing on a small platform.

Pinky is rocking Pinocchio couture complete with the iconic elongated nose and a sign, *MENTIRAS, #NAVAR-RORENUNCIA*. Sammy recognizes it as the popular phrase coined and used during the protests of twenty nineteen, intended to force the governor, Navarro, to resign from his post after the revelation of corrupt and unethical behavior. Pinky alternates from posing on her platform to strutting around the plaza voguing and calling for the homophobic and corrupt governor's resignation. She occasionally stops to chat with people, both fans and curious passerby's who listen carefully, smile, and offer emphatic gestures of support.

"*¡No más de tus mentiras, resigna y retira!* No more of your lies, retire and resign!"

As Pinky chants, people join in all around her. "*¡No más de tus mentiras, resigna y retira! ¡No más de tus mentiras, resigna y retira!*"

"Come on, it's starting." Valeria takes Sammy's hand.

Sammy lets Valeria lead him toward an individual with a megaphone, a shimmery mesh shirt, and pigtails made of different colored ribbons who is calling the crowd to attention.

"*¡Atención, mi gente! Bienvenides a todes*, welcome to the Haus of Resistance's debut performance. Thank you for coming out and using your proud *patería* to help cut off the head of that homophobic, corrupt snake, Navarro!"

"*¡Navarro Renuncia!*" A unified roar from the colorful sea of sequins, wigs, crop tops, bare flesh, and smiles sets off a frenzy of goosebumps on Sammy's body.

"You think we're trash, *gobernador*? Well, *cabrón*, I got news for you, this trash is gonna kick your pathetic ass right out of office."

"¡*Navarro Renuncia*!"

"In a few seconds, our performers are going to get this party started and Navarro is going to see exactly how gay we are. Let the *patería* begin!"

Pleneros begin playing their percussion instruments and emerge from the crowd in one united front. Other instruments join, the sound of *panderos,* sticks, and *güiros* echoing through the plaza. Valeria begins to throw it back, but Sammy hesitates.

"*Vente*, Papi. Let's dance," Valeria beckons Sammy.

Sammy begins to sway, and Valeria takes his hands. He looks around, no one seems to be staring. Sammy's movements get more purposeful and energetic. In a few seconds, his hips sway like all those hours of watching Shakira videos had taught him when he was really into the Colombian performer.

As Sammy and Valeria move in unison, they bump into something that throws off their rhythm. Sammy and Valeria turn to find five policemen.

"*Ay, disculpa*. I'm sorry, we got a little carried away and didn't see you there."

"Have you ladies been drinking today?" A cop with a beachball of a belly studies Valeria and Sammy's faces.

Sammy winces at the misgendering but doesn't correct it.

"What? No. We just got here, for your information."

Sammy looks at Valeria wide-eyed. What the hell is she doing?

"*La actitud no es necesaria*." The cop takes a step toward Valeria then looks back at his cohorts. "*Ya tu sabes*, you know how it is. They get a little booze in them, and bitches go crazy."

The other cops laugh. Sammy's hands begin to shake.

"Excuse me? What did you call us?"

"Okay, ma'am. I'm going to need you to take a step back and calm down."

"Calm down?"

Some people have taken notice of the skirmish and are

engaged watching the exchange between Valeria and the policeman. The pot-bellied cop grabs his walkie and holds it up to his face.

"This is Rivera, I'm at the Plaza de Armas and—"

An explosion resounds around the plaza making everyone jump. Then, a speaker roars to life playing "Born This Way" by Lady Gaga. The show is starting. Noticing the policemen are distracted, Sammy grabs Valeria's hand and leads her away from the cops and deeper into the safety of the crowd. Sammy watches as the policeman with the walkie looks around. Sammy and Valeria manage to remain out of sight while keeping an eye on the cop. Finally, they see the policeman put his walkie away. They watch as the policemen hang around for a minute, the one that had been arguing with Valeria looking hungry, desperate for something to pounce on and devour. Sammy and Valeria hide behind a wall of *cuirs* keeping an eye on the policemen who eventually lose interest and saunter away to another part of the plaza in search of new victims, no doubt. Sammy turns to Valeria with wide eyes and sighs vocally.

"Fuck me." Sammy wipes his brow, ridding it of the beads of sweat that had gathered.

Despite the confrontation, the show is still on. Transman and *cuir* performer Charlie is shirtless rocking skin-tight leather pants and prosthetic horns. It's fire demon realness. He expertly plays with fire, drawing oohs and awes from the crowd while dancers run around with signs that say things like *Siempre Pato, Nunca Pillo*, always gay, never a crook, and *Ni Corruptos Ni Cobardes*, we're neither corrupt nor cowardly. The crowd explodes into a frenzy when Charlie blows an epic fireball for his finale.

The crowd roars when Pinky steps out with her Pinocchio couture and #NAVARRORENUNCIA sign. She delivers an impassioned speech that begins with the story of transwoman Vanesa Quintero's tragic story and ends with a call to continue fighting for *cuir* rights and the rights of Puerto Ricans even after the governor leaves office. Pinky concludes her performance with a lip-sync of Marc Anthony's "Preciosa." The crowd joins in.

"That was incredible." Valeria skips through the parking lot.

"Totally, except I haven't been able to check my messages, and dad texted earlier. This gringa knocked my phone out of my hand, cracked it, and killed it."

"Inconsiderate jerk."

"Whatever, that was still amazing. Thanks for making me come."

"That's what I'm here for. Want to come with me to meet Graci? She's the one opening that *cuir* bar I told you about. I think it's just about done, and she said she could hook me up with a job. She might be able to hook you up too."

"I wish I could, but I should get home and see what's up with dad." Sammy rolls his eyes.

"You should be grateful. I would kill to have a supportive father. Mine hasn't spoken to me since I came out ten years ago."

Sammy hugs Valeria. "You're right. His concern just gets a bit annoying sometimes."

"Text me when you get home, *mi amor*."

"Have fun. Tell Graci I'm excited for Loverbar to open and I'm interested in a job." Sammy kisses Valeria on the cheek and gets in his car.

Sammy tries to be quiet as he inserts his house key in the lock, turns it, and pushes the door open.

Nice and quiet. Sammy slowly shuts the door and tiptoes toward his room down the hall past the living room. Sammy's father is sitting in the living room watching TV.

"*Buenas noches, pa.*" Sammy tries to walk away.

"Your grandmother is in the hospital."

Sammy stops in his tracks.

"I couldn't reach you."

"Is she okay?"

"For now."

Sammy walks to his father and hugs him.

"Papi, I'm sorry. My phone broke." Sammy shows his father the cracked phone, tears forming in his eyes.

They embrace for a minute in silence.

Sammy is not able to sleep all night. Thoughts of everything that could go wrong and how it's all his fault swirl around his head, a malicious twister of guilt and anxiety that won't let up. As soon as light appears through Sammy's window, he's up and ready to get to the hospital. His father offers to drive, and Sammy doesn't refuse. His hands haven't stopped shaking since he received the news about his *Abuelita* last night.

Sammy's hands are still shaking as they grasp the hospital room door handle. His palm immediately begins to sweat as he grips and pulls down releasing the lock and opening the door. His father follows him into the room and stands off to the side.

"*Abuelita?*" Sammy is relieved to find her propped up in the bed alive and alert as ever.

She gazes into the TV mounted on the wall before her which is playing a news story about yesterday's drag ball protest. Oh god. She knows. He feels his muscles tense.

"*Ay, mi estrella.* You finally made it." She raises and extends her wrinkled arms toward Sammy.

Sammy walks to her and hugs her carefully, the familiar scent of her filling his nostrils. Sammy disengages from the hug.

"*Abuelita, discúlpa.* I'm sorry. I didn't know you were in the hospital. My phone—"

"I know where you were, and there's no need to explain. Everything is going to be okay." She smiles taking Sammy's hands in hers.

Sammy returns the smile, the seed of hope. His muscles relax at the possibility of acceptance.

"It's not your fault, *es el diablo.* It's the devil making you lead this lifestyle. But don't worry, God is good. This is just something you're going through, *ya verás*, it's just a phase. Your great uncle went through it, too, but your great grandfather took him right to the church and they set him straight. He lived a perfectly normal life. Maybe your father can start looking into that. Everybody needs a little help turning away from the temptations of Satan sometimes."

Sammy pulls his hands out of his grandmothers'. Both Sammy and his grandmother look at Sammy's father expectantly. He stands silent and motionless, eyes wide, darting back and forth between his mother and his son. Sammy slowly shakes his head at his father. He can feel the bile in his empty stomach threatening to emerge as his sight grows hazy behind tears. He backs up from his father and grand-mother. His face is boiling, and he wants to scream. Sammy shakes, containing the urge and brings himself down to a simmer.

"*Abuelita*, I love you but you're a terrible person." Sammy made for the door. He turns to face his father. "And you—¿*Tú sabes qué? Pichea*." He sighs. "Forget it."

"¿*Y esa falta de respeto*? ¡*Ay santo*! Why are you trying to kill me when all I'm trying to do is save your soul!" His *Abuelita* clutches her chest.

Sammy opens his mouth to respond but stops when his father raises a hand, a gesture Sammy's father has always used to demand silence. His father turns to face the old woman still clutching her chest in the hospital bed.

"Don't ever speak to my son like that again." Sammy's father slowly walks past the hospital bed and opens the door. "I'll be back later, mom."

The old woman's jaw drops, her hands finally abandoning her chest. She scoffs, crosses her arms, and turns away from her family. Sammy's father is still holding the door open. He makes eye contact with his son.

"Let's go, Sammy."

Chapter Seven

Rhythmic Resistance

"So, how was it?" Pinky says poking Valeria repeatedly.

Valeria slaps away her prodding finger with a smile.

"Well, let's just say he was not okay with my truth. I barely got out of there with my face intact." Valeria chuckles, but her hands shake as she remembers that night.

Valeria gave herself a final look in the mirror and headed out. Her date was on time, which was very impressive. Most guys arrive an hour plus late stating only *que se atrasaron*, they got held up. He was all the tall, dark, and handsome the fairytales promised, the fairytales Valeria figured she would never fit into. His name was Fernando. Valeria always liked that name. To her, it radiated royalty.

Old San Juan was packed that Friday, as usual. They went to dinner at seafood place on Recinto Sur Street. Seafood is Valeria's favorite, and she found it oddly charming when Ferdinando made remarks about his really being in the mood for fish tonight, wink, wink. A few cocktails, some fried red snapper, and a mixed seafood salad with *tostones* later, Valeria was his. They walked back to his car hand in hand. Once they arrived, Fernando made his move, and Valeria fell into his kiss.

"I don't usually do this on the first date, but would you want to come to my next show?"

"You perform? Very cool. Dancer, actor?"

Valeria swallowed hard.

"I'm a drag performer."

Ferdinando immediately separated from Valeria.

"*¿Qué tu dices?*" Louder. "What are you saying?" His eyes widened. "Are you a—" As the realization sank in, Ferdinando paced, his face getting increasingly red.

Valeria watches, her mind racing for the right words to say.

"I'm sorry, I—"

Ferdinando slams a hand onto the car centimeters from her face.

"I should kill you, *jodío maricón*. Fucking faggot."

"*Ay, mi amor*. Are you okay?"

Pinky's words bring Valeria back.

"Oh, yeah. I'm fine." Valeria waves away Pinky's concern but can't keep from remembering the sound of the man's hand slamming into the car centimeters from her cheek, his face contorted in rage.

"Maybe next time, tell them your truth before meeting up?" Pinky attempts eye contact with Valeria who evades, her gaze fixed to the floor.

If Valeria tells them the truth, they'll never give her a chance.

"Well, anyway, we're in, right?" Pinky asks.

Valeria looks up at the change of subject. Valeria and Pinky have attended every protest so far despite the beating they took during the first one. Valeria is quiet for a moment remembering the expanse of time she was lost in the yellow fog, anonymous limbs pushing and shoving as she struggled to find Pinky. The second protest was the opposite, a total love fest that left Valeria feeling full and satisfied. This third one, to be determined.

"Of course, we're in. If that misogynist *cuir* basher stays in office, we will have more Alexa's on our hands?" The image of transwoman Alexa gunned-down corpse flashes in Valeria's mind.

Valeria shakes her head but fails to rid herself of the vision. A few months ago, people called the cops on Alexa for entering the women's bathroom in a McDonald's restaurant. They said she was a threat to the other women. That's why she was gunned down, for entering a restroom.

Valeria's phone dings, it's a text.

Mira belleza, when do I finally get to meet you in person?

It's the new guy she's been texting, Manuel. Valeria smiled, but it quickly fades when Alexa and her last date reenter her thoughts. Valeria picks at her nails staring blankly ahead. She has a bit of tough skin where her thumbnail meets her finger that she is very focused on removing. Pinky slides

Valeria her phone across the kitchen table. Valeria desists chewing on her thumb and studies the information on the phone screen.

Perreo Combativo 24 de Julio 2019 / 9 PM La Fortelza.

Combative dirty dancing, a dance protest. Would Manuel find more to protest?

"Do you mind if I ask this new guy along?"

"Damn, girl. Where do you find all of these guys?"

"Just my unrelenting charm, I suppose." Valeria runs her hands through the long, brown hair she is so proud of, it took time and pricy conditioners, but it was worth it.

Pinky chuckles.

"Get that multitasking, girl. Date and protest at the same time."

Valeria smiles, nods then drops her gaze to the floor, her leg starts bouncing.

"Do you think people will be as welcoming as they were at the drag ball protest?" Valeria asks.

Pinky leans back in her chair and sighs. "Does it matter?"

"I guess not. It would just be nice not to be scared for once." Valeria chuckles, her leg still bouncing.

Valeria looks at herself in the mirror as she applies her makeup. Her phone dings indicating a message. It's Manuel.

Hola belleza tropical, 10 pm tonight, yeah?

Valeria feels her insides tingle as she confirms their meet-up time. With a smile, she continues putting on her face. She visualizes her and Manuel walking hand in hand and cuddling on couches, going to concerts and having lazy brunches on Sunday with their friends after a night of partying at the club. All the things she's never had the opportunity to do with a partner.

The eyeliner is proving difficult to apply. Her hand won't stop shaking. Her face inches from the mirror, she tries to steady herself and begins applying a thin, black line to her left eyelid.

He's going to be cool, *lo sé*. Not like that asshole Fernando.

"Ouch!"

Valeria accidentally pokes herself in the eye with the eyeliner. Great, now she looks like she has pink eye. She fans her eye for a bit and gets it to settle down some. Once she is done with her makeup, it's time to tuck. Testicles in hand, she prepares to gently slide them into place when a ding alerts her of another message from Manuel.

Tienes tremendo cuerpazo. I can't wait to see that beautiful body in person.

He thinks I have an amazing body? Valeria feels her heartbeat stutter.

Testes still in hand, she reads the message then finishes tucking them away. She begins typing a response.

Hey, there's something I should tell you—

Valeria stops typing and erases the message. Her phone rings, making Valeria jump. It's Pinky.

"Hey, girl, what's the plan?" Pinky asks. "Now that the governor has announced that he will finally be addressing the public, I'm not sure what the deal is with the dance protest. You think he's going to resign?"

"It's still on, as far as I know, and I hope so." Valeria looks at herself in the mirror and fusses with her hair.

"Bring it on. I'm ready to get down and grind in protest, celebration, or whatever the outcome of the speech calls for."

Valeria smiles as Pinky's fierce energy translates through the phone.

"I'm supposed to meet the guy there at ten, so why don't we meet at nine by La Puntilla."

"Have you been upfront with—"

"See you there, *te amo*." Valeria briskly hangs up the phone. After all, the matter can be postponed for a little while, right?

When Valeria arrives in Old San Juan for the dance protest, Pinky is not there yet. She stands on the same corner at the entrance of La Puntilla parking lot where the Uber driver left her, waiting. Old San Juan is already packed, just like the Friday of her last date. Valeria looks around shifting her weight from left to right.

Come on, Pinky. Don't make me wait here alone.

An interminable line of vehicles runs down the docks and out of the city, Puerto Rico's hip-hop nation ready to party and protest. The cobble-stoned streets slowly flood with *reggaetoneros* sporting flat-billed caps, Jordan sneakers, diamond stud earrings, and chains, classic reggaeton chic. Growing up, Valeria's parents insisted that reggaeton es *música sucia de mala influencia,* dirty music that is a bad influence. That's probably what made it the perfect genre for a dance protest against a bigoted governor. Valeria would listen to it in secret and daydream about bumping and grinding with those delicious street-thug types that blasted reggaeton from the souped-up speakers of their foreign-made cars. Why are straight boys always the sexiest?

The energy at the *Perreo Combativo* dance protest was high and electric like that felt when walking with a crowd of hundreds of fans toward a concert. Signs calling for the governor's resignation float around the crowd bobbing up and down like a buoy in rough waters. It feels different than the drag ball. Some people walk right by Valeria without paying attention, but others fixate on her a bit too long. They probably fixated on Alexa like that too. It makes her heart palpitate. She hopes Pinky left on time.

Valeria searches in her purse for her phone, but it's a black hole. She rummages through the collection of makeup, keys, pens, and other miscellaneous objects that hold her phone hostage. As she searches, someone bearhugs her from behind. Valeria jumps and thrashes.

"¡*Suéltame*! Let me go."

They release her.

"*Tranquila,* calm down, it's just me."

Valeria turns to find Pinky standing with her arms up, suggesting a guilty as charged attitude. A sigh escapes Valeria's lips as her shoulders relax.

"I'm sorry, *mala mía.* My bad. I'm just excited. Or maybe anxious? I can't tell, this is a crap ton of people." Pinky motions to the choppy ocean of people around her.

Valeria looks around. The volume of people is beginning to cause pushing and shoving among the hordes of wanna-be gangsters. The side-eyeing and furrowed brows of the men around her make Valeria tremble.

Pinky notices Valeria tense and gives her a playful shove.

"Come on, let's try to be positive." Pinky takes hold of Valeria's arm and ushers her forward. "I'll admit, there's not the same vibe as the drag ball, but these are our people too, *todes boricuas*. Yeah, all Puerto Rican. Does that make her fear any less valid? "We've been dropping it like it's hot just as long as all of them have, and we have a right to be here."

By the time they reach the Plaza de la Monjas, the rhythmic protest is in full swing. Valeria can't tell where one sweaty body begins and the other ends as hundreds roll and thrust their hips to the sound of Residente's "Bellacoso." Valeria and Pinky dance their way through the crowd, a trick every Puerto Rican knows thanks to the annual San Sebastián Festival where, somehow, the entire island fits into the northwest triangle of Old San Juan. Valeria feels her phone vibrate and checks her messages.

Estoy llegando a la plaza. Where are you?

It's Manuel, almost to the plaza. Valeria smiles, typing her response.

"I'm assuming that smile means he's here," Pinky says while dancing.

Ten minutes later, Valeria's date arrives.

"Your pictures don't do you justice." Valeria's date looks her up and down.

Valeria's face grows warm and her cheeks blush.

So far so good.

"I'm Pinky, the one who will kill you if you hurt her." Pinky steps between them, extending a hand.

He smiles and returns the handshake. "Manuel."

Pinky looks him up and down before turning her attention to a *papisongo*, a sexy man, who has his eye on her.

"You two have fun, now. Mama's hungry and she needs a little snack." Pinky winks at them and dances toward the man ogling her.

Not many words are exchanged before Valeria and Manuel get to it. At first, Valeria's movements are subtle. All the fantasies of house parties and garage grinding that were her saving grace during her adolescence scroll through her mind, a nostalgic slideshow. Valeria closes her eyes and tries to get lost in the moment but Manuel's rhythmless hip thrusts make it difficult. She tries guiding him with her movements, but he does not seem to catch her moves. The awkward dancing continues, as Valeria struggles to stay on beat with an off-beat partner.

"Let's get closer to the stage," Valeria says, turning to Manuel.

Manuel nods and lets Valeria lead him by the hand. Maybe being closer to the DJ will motivate him to be smoother. She looks around for Pinky to let her know they're moving but can't find her in the heaving mass. Valeria and Manuel make it to the stage where the DJ vibes with the crowd. Valeria and Manuel, on the other hand, are still struggling. He's somehow dancing worse than before and now he's knocking Valeria off balance. Valeria finally reaches behind her and takes hold of his hips.

"*Sígueme*, follow me," Valeria says, forcing his hips to move from side to side on beat.

He finally responds and slows down, falling more in sync with Valeria. It's not perfect, but it's a start. Valeria bites her lip reveling in the fact that he finally let her take the lead. His hands on her hips occasionally wander a bit too far igniting Valeria. It starts in her loins and grows and grows until it takes hold of everything.

"*¿Dónde están las nenas*? Where my girls at?" the DJ says into the mic.

A thunderous response emanates from the crowd. The DJ looks down approvingly from his podium.

"For this next song, I'm going to need a couple of honeys on stage with me."

Girls rush the stage and start to climb on.

"*Vengo ahora*, watch and learn." Valeria winks at Manuel and mounts the stage. She takes her place and gets to it.

"Lost you there for a while."

"She appears. Where were you?"

Pinky is covered in sweat and smiling from ear to ear. She climbs on stage with Valeria.

"Lost in the bodies, baby."

Valeria laughs.

Valeria and Pinky start dancing. They are each other's perfect partners, eight years in the making. Manuel watches, looking like a cartoon wolf losing his shit at the sight of attractive girls, eyes bulging out, drool threatening to trickle from his agape mouth.

"*¡Mi gente*! The governor is about to talk. It's going

down," the DJ says into the microphone.

The people in the crowd cheer and hurriedly turn their attention to their phones. Valeria and Pinky do the same.

Good evening, Puerto Rico.

I've always done my best to contribute to the wellbeing of my island and my people. I've also always taken pride in owning up to my misakes.

"Oh my God, it's actually happening," Pinky says, her eyes widening.

Navarro's ongoing resignation speech brings the girls on stage to a whole new level, and the DJ, as if taking their cue, transitions to Bad Bunny's feminist reggaeton anthem "Yo Perreo Sola." They all seem to be connected as they move in sync, every woman with the same screw-you-I-make-the-rules expression on their heavily made-up and sweaty faces.

Manuel gazes up from the crowd. He doesn't take his eyes off Valeria, and Valeria loves it. She notices people lean in and briefly speak to Manuel. He smiled, nods, and occasionally points to Valeria on stage with a smile and a wink. So, this is what it feels like for someone to be proud to be seen with you? Valeria's whole body catches fire making her feel invincible. Then, as if possessed by both Athena and Aphrodite, a hybrid warrior seductress, Valeria removes her top and the women on stage follow suit, freeing their bosom.

"Siempre puta, nunca pilla," Valeria says, thrusting her fist in the air.

The crowd turns its attention from the governor's speech to the bare-breasted ladies on stage. Flashes and recording lights pepper the audience, as contemporary society's need to document and post takes control. Valeria continues to dance getting increasingly sensual and aggressive while Pinky winds down and finally stops moving.

"I'm getting off stage. You should come with me," Pinky covers herself up.

"What?" Valeria turns and sees Pinky waiting for her at the edge of the stage.

She spots Manuel in the crowd but is unable to make eye

contact. He is too busy looking around and listening to whatever people are saying. The women around her keep dancing
as Bad Bunny's voice continues blaring on the speakers. Was
the music this loud before?

Valeria watches as a look of realization and rage dawn on
Manuel's face. He turns from the stage and hurries away.
Valeria hops off the stage and follows.

"Manuel. Manuel!" He either can't hear her or chooses
not to.

When she finally reaches him, she grabs his arm.

"Hey. *¿Qué pasa?* Where are you going?"

Manuel violently shakes her hand off his arm.

"Don't ever contact me again. You're lucky we're in
public." The face that was soft and wanting just minutes
before is hard and defensive.

"Please, just give me a—" Valeria reaches after him.

Manuel turns and raises a fist. Valeria jumps back, turns
away, and raises her hands to protect her face. She waits for
the blow. She knew this would eventually happen. What did
she expect? She waits and waits but it doesn't come. When
she opens her eyes, Manuel has disappeared into the crowd.

"Coward!" Valeria says to the spot where Manuel had
been standing.

Valeria struggles to keep from crying, as her chest heaves
and heaves. Fernando, Alexa's death, and Manuel circulate
her thoughts. The crowd bumps and shoves Valeria as the
dancing continues around her. Her hands won't stop shaking,
and she has no idea where Pinky is. Her chest heaves faster
and faster.

"Baby, did you hear? We did it, he resigned!"

Valeria turns to find Pinky. Pinky's excitement turns to
concern when she sees Valeria's face.

"What happened? Did he . . ."

"No."

"What did he—?"

"He's gone."

Pinky notices Valeria's heaving chest and shaking hands.

"Let's get out of here." Pinky leads Valeria away from
the crowd.

Once in Pinky's car, tears finally begin silently streaming

down Valeria's face.

"Do you want to talk about it?"

Valeria shakes her head.

"Okay. Let me know if you change your mind."

Valeria reaches out and places a hand on Pinky's thigh.

"*Gracias.*"

Pinky takes hold of Valeria and squeezes her tight. They release each other when Valeria's phone goes off.

"Maybe it's him."

Valeria checks her phone hoping Pinky is right but it's just her friend Sammy checking in.

Hey, how's the date?

Valeria throws her phone on the floorboards.

For the first few days after the protest, Valeria checks her phone hoping to see a message from Manuel. So stupid. Screw it, she's used to it anyway. Plus, the governor is gone. Valeria should be happy.

Mid pep talk, her phone rings. Her heart flutters at the possibility that Manuel is not, in fact, a complete jackass and is calling to apologize, but it's Pinky. Reality bites.

"Turn the tv on and put it on Mega TV. La Comay is talking about the protest."

Valeria does so and watches. The Comay looks ridiculous as ever. It blew Valeria's mind that one of Puerto Rico's most popular shows and main source of gossip is a gaudy, female puppet with scarecrow hair and a man's hand shoved up her ass. Valeria listens as the puppet rattles on.

"*Habían muchachas allí perreando, en la iglesia.* There were women dancing provocatively, right there in front of the church."

"*Ay Señor,*" her male co-star and co-host, Rocky, says.

"Mira, you're not going to believe it, *pero algunas de esas mujeres* were practically naked. with their bosoms exposed."

"Naked?" Rocky says. "In front of the cathedral?"

"Yes, *eso es así.*"

"*Ay, Señor,*" Rocky says again, this time crossing himself. "God bless those girls."

"*Señoras y señores,* we are going to show the video. Obviously, we had to censor the women's breasts *porque imagínese."*

"Sacrilegio!"

"Eso es así, absolutely. Let's go ahead play it. A*delante, adelante."*

Valeria watches herself on screen, her face expressionless. Pinky had already leaped off stage, it is Valeria that is front and center. Her hands shake as she watches.

The conversation between La Comay and Rocky continues with a few more guilt trips about respectability, and then the segment is through. Valeria sighs deeply.

"Mi amor, are you okay?"

Valeria remains silent for another few seconds.

"Yeah, I'm fine, just embarrassed. We seriously need Loverbar to open so I can dance and meet guys in peace. Nice guys that don't want to bash my face in."

"Well, your face is safe for now, and at least La Comay gendered you correctly."

Valeria's phone buzzes.

"Hold on, Pink. I got a text." Valeria checks the message. "Who is it?"

Just a guy I met a few weeks ago. He wants to go out."

"Does he know the truth, nothing but the truth, so help you gay god?"

"No, but he's about to."

Chapter Eight

Slow Service

She reads the words again making sure she didn't imagine them.

"We're pleased to offer you a Teaching Assistantship for the 2019-2020 academic year starting September 1, 2019—"

Mabel twirls her ponytail with her left hand while staring at the acceptance letter on the computer screen. When she got accepted into the Public Policy and Administration Doctoral Program in the U.S., she swore she wouldn't accept unless she got financial assistance. She doesn't need any more debt.

Mabel waited all day to read the letter when she got the notification. Sitting on her bed in the dead of night, she logged into the university portal with shaking hands. "We're pleased—" Mabel cried reading the words.

Now, rereading the letter, Mabel wants to cry again. She sighs, shuts off the computer, and walks to the window of her studio apartment. Her mother thought the place too small, but after three years, Mabel still believes the view is worth the lack of space. Waking up and seeing the beach in the distance is priceless. There are also the pelicans she's grown fond of seeing perched on the treetops right outside her apartment. She'd miss them.

Mabel's phone buzzes, it's a text from Lisandra.

"Hey, beautiful, I'll be visiting you at work today after the protest. *Te amo*."

Mabel's smiles, warmth filling her body. She goes to type a response, but stops, frowns, and puts the phone down. What would Lisandra say? She'd be happy, of course, and urge Mabel to accept the assistantship that will allow her to pursue her doctoral studies free of charge on the U.S. mainland. Out there, her academic career wouldn't be delayed due to constant power outages and incessant student strikes, but she would have to leave the island, her life, her home. Mabel leans on the windowsill and runs both hands through her curly, brown hair. This has been Mabel's dream since she was a young undergraduate at the University of Puerto Rico at Rio Piedras. But what about Lisandra? Long distance is a fool's game, she knew from experience. She and Norma had a nasty falling out a few years ago.

Norma was older than Mabel. She had finished her bachelor's degree a year before her. The second Norma was out of school, she got an offer to work with her uncle in Pennsylvania, and the salary and benefits she'd receive there are much more impressive than what she could hope to receive on the bankrupt island. Mabel was happy for her, and for a second believed they could make it work, but after a few months of being separated, things started to change. Norma wouldn't answer the phone because she was busy, and eventually, they were down to one unenthusiastic conversation a week. Mabel confronted her about it, desperate to save what they once had, but Norma didn't seem to think it was worth saving. Norma wanted to focus on her new life. Now, they aren't even friends on social media. That, however, is Mabel's doing. It hurt too much to see Norma enjoying herself while Mabel nursed a breakup. She didn't want her relationship with Lisandra to end up like that.

The wind blows carrying its salty seaside scent into Mabel's nostrils. She breathes it in and looks at her phone. It's eleven, if she doesn't get going, she'll be late for her shift.

Xavi is already there when she arrives. Although there technically isn't a manager at the fusion restaurant where she works, everyone knows it's Xavi. That place can't run without him.

"*Buenos días*, baby boo." Xavi smiles, as he polishes glasses behind the bar.

Mabel returns the smile. "What's up, buttercup?"

They met at one of Lola Love's drag shows before the protests against the governor, before Hurricane María, before everything went to shit. At least that jerk Navarro is out of office now.

"It's supposed to get busy later today. A few of the bars on San Sebastián street are throwing parties to celebrate Navarro resigning."

"Hooray for tips but screw the traffic we're going to have

to deal with."

Xavi chuckles. "We can always have a drink until it dies down."

"You read my mind."

Mabel puts her apron on and joins Xavi behind the bar.

"What do you need?"

"Can you make sure the miso and salad are ready in the back? I don't want a repeat of the February Friday Night Fiasco."

That was easily the worst dinner service they had ever had thanks to Gian's lazy ass. Anytime he was on shift, something went wrong.

"I got you," Mabel says, heading to the kitchen.

Pedro, the head cook, is busy prepping. The smell of *sofrito*, finely chopped onions, garlic, and pepper, make Mabel's mouth water. It doesn't matter that this is a Japanese and Chinese fusion restaurant, Pedro always cooks with *sofrito*, so Puerto Rican. The owner, Kiko, always gets onto him about it, but never makes him stop. Secretly, Kiko knows that's why people love the food so much.

"Smells good."

"*Belleza, buenos días*," Pedro says while slicing some onions. "*¿Estás* ready? I'm told we're going to get swamped today."

"You know me, I was born ready."

Pedro smiles. Despite his three missing teeth, Mabel always sees him around town with a lady on his arm.

"That's why you're my favorite. Don't tell Xavi I said that."

"Your secret is safe with me." Mabel walks to where they keep the soups and salads. They're good on salads, but they're running low on miso.

"Need some help with the miso?"

"*Si, por favor.*"

Mabel grabs the miso paste, vegetable broth, onion, tofu, and mushrooms and gets to work.

"Pedro, if you had the chance to be head chef at a really nice restaurant in the states, would you go?"

"Depends. How much am I making?"

"Much more than you make here."

"Hmm." Pedro furrows his thick brow. "I don't know. I'd have to leave everything and start again. Plus, the ladies love me here. I'm not sure what the *gringas* would think of me."

Mabel laughs. She'd miss Pedro.

"What about you?" Pedro fixes his gaze on Mabel.

She looks at Pedro, then refocuses on the half-made soup. "I don't want to be a chef, so."

"*¿Estás chistosa hoy?* You got jokes today? Didn't you apply to some fancy school or something? What if you get in? Will you go?"

Mabel silently stirs the soup before her, swirling the miso paste into white spirals.

"Okay, okay. I can take a hint." Pedro gets back to the onions.

Mabel finishes the miso and covers the tub with the metallic lid that keeps it warm.

"Do you need anything else?"

Pedro looks at Mabel. "No, I'm good."

Mabel moves to leave the kitchen.

"*Mira*, for what it's worth, just because leaving isn't for me, doesn't mean it isn't for you."

Mabel smiles weakly and leaves the kitchen. Xavi is done with the bar and has moved on to setting the tables.

"What's with the sour puss today?" Xavi asks without looking up.

He has the rather creepy ability to read a person's energy without even looking at them. "Is Pedro hitting on you again?"

Mabel laughs. "No, just thinking."

"About?"

Mabel knows what Xavi will say, the same thing Lisandra would say. Would anyone ask her to stay?

"I don't want to bore you with my existential bullshit. How's dating been since He-Who-Must-Not-Be-Named?"

"Ugh, don't even get me started."

"Uh-oh, not great?"

"Everyone seems so thirsty, and I'm still traumatized from that jerk-off cheating."

"I don't blame you. At least he went to jail for a bit." Mabel laughs recalling the incident Xavi recounted involving his ex-boyfriend's insistence that they hike to a beach through private property.

The thought of Xavi, who never works out, running like a bat out of hell from the cops through a mess of sand, palm trees, and vegetation is hilarious.

"True that. Now, I just need the balls to get back out there."

"If you ever want me to come out with you, I can totally wingman. Plus, a little moral support and backup are always good."

Xavi smiled. "I'm going to take you up on that."

"Now, back to you. Don't think I've forgotten about your sour puss. What's going on?"

Xavi never skips a beat.

"*Bueno*, yesterday I got—"

Two women saunter into the restaurant dressed and ready to party. The women have fresh blowouts, mini dresses, and what Mabel calls fuck me heels. They must be celebrating something.

"*Buenas*, take a seat anywhere you'd like," Mabel says.

Xavi sighs. "This conversation isn't finished, young lady."

Mabel sticks her tongue out and heads to the duo's table.

"Hey, can I get you guys something to drink? Maybe a little mojito to get the party juices flowing?"

The ladies giggle. It's this type of charm that made Mabel a successful waitress.

"Yes, girl, you know what's up," one of the women said.

"You got it." Mabel heads to the bar where Xavi already has two mojito glasses prepped.

"You're welcome." Xavi winks at her.

"You're such an eavesdropper."

"It's called anticipation and attention to detail. You should try it sometime."

"Oh, is that so?" Mabel pinches Xavi, making him jump.

"Stop it!" He slaps her hand away, trying not to laugh. "So unprofessional."

"You know you love me." Mabel gets to work muddling mint leaves, lime wedges, and sugar in the glasses.

"And I haven't forgotten. What's on your mind that

you're working so hard to keep from me?"

"Remember that public policy program I applied to?"

"Of course. What happened? You didn't get in?"

"Actually, it's the opposite. I got in, and I got the assistantship. My tuition will be paid for if I accept."

"What? That's incredible. Congratulations."

He swiftly takes Mabel in his arms and twirls her around. She struggles in protest making Xavi release her.

"Yeah, thanks."

"But you're not happy about it. What the hell, Mabel?"

"What about Lisandra? My life here?"

"What about your dreams and how much you could do with that doctoral degree?"

Mabel rolls her eyes, grabs the completed mojitos, and heads to the table.

The ladies accept the drinks with smiles and promptly place their order, Chef Sushi Special for two.

"Ready for the weekend?" Mabel asks one of the women.

"That obvious, huh?"

"The blowouts gave you away." Mabel winks.

The ladies giggle at Mabel's flirtation.

"We're celebrating Tamara getting a dope position at a firm in D.C. So, if you could bring a celebratory brownie at the end, that would be great."

Tamara smiles. "You don't need to tell everyone we meet today, Carol."

"Yes, I do. I'm proud of you. It's not like you could get a job here. Plus, you're going to be working with immigrants. Speaking up for the little guy, and that shit is fucking heroic." Carol hugs Tamara whose cheeks flushed.

"That's awesome, congratulations," Mabel said, forcing a smile and tapping her pen on the notepad she uses to take orders. "Think you'll ever come back?"

Tamara thinks for a minute. "I'd like to, but I don't see why I would. There's nothing for me here, career wise."

Mabel nods.

"Enjoy those mojitos, and I'll be back soon with that sushi."

Mabel quickly walks into the bathroom and locks the door. She goes to a stall, unzips her black work pants, and forces them down her curvaceous legs until they're at her ankles. Down go the undies, and she takes a seat. She stares at her undies. It's the Flash-themed pair Lisandra gave her for Valentine's Day. Lisandra still hadn't texted her back. She replied with, 'Okay. See you later, *te amo*' and puts the phone away, quickly quelling the temptation to tell Lisandra everything by text. Textual impulsivity never helped anyone. No, this is an in-person conversation. Not that Mabel had any doubt about what Lisandra would say.

Could Mabel be one of those people that gives up everything for their goals? It's not like she'd be gone forever. She'd come back, she always told herself. Once she got the Ph.D., she'd come back and put it to use bettering the socio-political conditions on the island, if she could find a position. All the budget cuts and the political climate were very disheartening, it's no wonder people are leaving in droves.

A knock on the door made Mabel jump.

"Yeah, sorry, coming."

She quickly finishes her business, washes her hands and face, and unlocks the door. It's Xavi.

"Are you okay? I'm sorry if I came on too strong. I'm just excited for you."

"I know." Mabel smiled.

"Lisandra is going to be excited for you, too."

Mabel's smile fades. "I know."

"Well, let future Mabel deal with that. Right now, we have to be ready for the rush."

Mabel nods and follows Xavi into the dining room.

After Tamara and Carol leave, another pair come in, a man and a woman. It's Xavi who greets this time.

"*Bienvenidos, donde gusten.* Take a seat wherever you'd like."

Xavi walks close and Mabel waits by the bar at the ready. She wants to have their drink order prepped by the time Xavi gets to her. She'll show Xavi anticipation.

"What are we drinking?" Xavi asks with a smile.

"Do you have *Gasolina*?"

Xavi stares back at him in silence as if to say, 'Are you for real?' With affordable pricing and seven to eleven percent alcohol content, *Gasolina* is a ready-made cocktail served in a pouch like an adult Capri Sun.

"*Disculpa*, sorry, but we don't have *Gasolina*. How about a house Sangría? They are the happy-hour favorite around here."

The man nods, satisfied. Mabel, who has been listening, gets two Sangría glasses out and fills them with fruit and ice.

"How's that for anticipation?"

Xavi laughs. "Not bad, not bad."

"Maybe we should start carrying *Gasolina*."

"Oh God, please. Kiko can barely handle Pedro's *sofrito*. His bougie ass would have a fit."

After the *Gasolina* table leaves, three hours pass with no guests.

Mabel and Xavi decide to play Hangman on cocktail napkins while they wait for the supposed rush. Using her vowel-first strategy, Mabel destroys Xavi the first few rounds.

"Whatever. I didn't stand a chance against you, doctor."

Mable squints her eyes and gives him the look.

"Okay, okay. I won't say another word until you tell me you're ready to talk about it."

They begin another round of Hangman.

"So." Xavi tries to act casual but fails. "Lisi is coming by later, right?"

Mable launches the look again.

"Graci is coming with her, that's why I know." Xavi manages to repel the accusatory stare.

"Yeah, they should be here once Lisi gets off work."

Mabel struggles to guess the right letters this round. There's an a and no e. What could it be? So many consonants, so little limbs. She shuffles through five-letter words in her head. Scare? Brave? Mabel decides to try r.

"People will come eat before they start partying. We will get slammed after for sure," Xavi ensures Mabel, whose only concern is guessing the five-letter word.

"I don't know, Kiko said the same thing during the festival of *Las Calles de San Sebastián*, and we got a whopping total of five tables that evening."

The r works out for Mabel. Now, what should she guess next?

"Let's be optimistic. I need the money so I can afford

school."

Mabel finally looks up from the game. She knows how much that degree in event planning means to Xavi and how little his ex supported that dream.

"Okay, the Law of Attraction, right? If we think it and believe it, it will happen."

"Right." Xavi forced a smile.

A crowd of chattering people storm by the restaurant, their smiling faces and enthusiastic gestures demonstrating Friday night excitement. So much possibility, so much fun. Xavi and Mabel stand. Maybe all that chattering and excitement made them hungry? They watch longingly as the crowd walks by. Xavi sighs.

"It's pointless. Let's face it. No tips tonight." He plops into a chair.

Mabel sits next to Xavi and shoves the cocktail napkin with their unfinished Hangman game toward him. As they're about to restart the game, the restaurant door flings open. A gust of wind follows Lisandra and Graci into the restaurant sending a few napkins into the air like white specs in a snow globe. Mabel stares at Lisandra as she makes her entrance. Her cocoa skin, midnight hair, and green eyes always leave Mabel breathless.

"Graci!" Xavi jumps up and runs to Graci who welcomes him with open arms.

Xavi had once told Mabel that he's inspired by Graci's ongoing struggle with sobriety. The fact that Graci was still on track to open her bar—yes, bar—made her an OG in his eyes. Graci has an unapologetic presence about her that is intoxicating.

"Xavi, how are you? Is Lola ready for her next gig? You know I'm going to want her performing at Loverbar."

Xavi smiles. "She's ready. It's getting her there on time that's going to be a challenge. When do you open again?"

"Next month if all goes well."

"That's so exciting." Xavi hugs Graci again. "I'm so proud of you, baby."

"Thanks." Graci's eyes water. "I am too."

"If you need my help with anything, let me know." Xavi puts a hand to his heart. "I got you."

"Hey, you." Lisandra looks at Mabel who's still sitting with the Hangman cocktail napkin in hand.

Mabel had not stopped staring at Lisandra since she came in.

"Hola." Mabel smiles and looks down at the floor, her stomach aflutter.

Even after a year of dating, Lisandra still made her jittery. Mabel walks to Lisandra and kisses her.

"How was work?"

"Normal, people won't stop talking about Navarro resigning." Lisandra shrugged her shoulders.

"Like that will fix anything. We need a complete overhaul of the administration." Graci shook her head.

"Come sit down." Xavi ushered them to a table. "The usual?"

"Yes, please," Lisandra and Graci responded in unison.

Xavi serves them up some Shirley Temples, virgin, of course. Mabel sat next to Lisandra and listened as her love and Graci continued discussing the extensive corruption of the Puerto Rican and the U.S. administrations. Mabel found Lisandra's revolutionary spirit very hot. Every time she spoke of independence and overthrowing the government, Mabel was overwhelmed by the desire to jump her bones. Mabel often wondered if her ambition of acquiring her Ph.D. in the states bothered Lisandra. After all, according to her, the U.S. administrations had a massive role in landing Puerto Rico in debt. Does running to the states for better opportunities make Mabel a traitor in Lisandra's eyes?

Lisandra's passion for politics and social justice is what drew Mabel to her in the first place. It all started a year ago when Mabel decided to attend a boycott at the University of Puerto Rico at Rio Piedras. Students were protesting a raise in tuition as well the cancellation of various degree programs. Lisandra was one of the speakers, that student behind the megaphone firing up the crowd demanding justice. Mabel was entranced. It didn't take her long to decide that she would introduce herself after the boycott and invite Lisandra out for some coffee.

"I love what you said today," Mabel said, latte in hand.

"Thanks, and thanks for coming." Lisandra sipped her black coffee.

"Do you think the administration will listen, or is education doomed to a steady decline? Not to be a pessimist."

"Oh, no." Lisandra gently touched Mabel's thigh. "It's a fair question to ask." Lisandra sat back in her chair and sighed. "I'm not sure they'll ever listen, but we have to keep trying. That's the only way change will come."

Mabel and Lisandra sipped their beverages.

"What do you think it will take? You know, for them to listen."

Lisandra thought for a moment. "Self-determination, and a complete overhaul of the administration."

Mabel nodded. "I couldn't agree more."

"Now we just have to make it happen, but that's a tall-ass order."

"If you're on the case, there's definitely hope," Mabel said, winking.

Lisandra's cheeks turned red.

Mabel smiled at the memory, wishing she could go back to that day, that beginning. After Graci and Lisandra downed an appetizer, Xavi invited Graci out for a quick cigarette. He locks eyes with Mabel, as he heads out the door. This time it's Xavi that gives her the look.

"What's up with you?" Lisandra said, taking advantage of the fact that they're alone.

"Huh?"

"You're acting weird, distant."

"Oh, I'm sorry."

"You don't need to apologize." Lisandra smiles and strokes Mabel's cheek. "Just tell me what's up."

Mabel placed her hand on top of Lisandra's.

"I got the assistantship." Mabel's heart pounds away in her chest.

Surely, Lisandra can hear it. Lisandra's eyes widened and welled up until tears threatened to spill over. She threw her arms around Mabel and squeezed.

"I'm so proud of you." Lisandra whispers. "Y—you have to go."

Mabel felt Lisandra's body tremble.

"What about us, our plans?" Mabel's voice shook. "Changing the island together?"

"It's not like you won't come back, and we can handle a bit of distance." Lisandra takes Mabel's hands in hers. "Plus, a fancy Ph.D. in public policy will help our plans to change things here."

Lisandra smiled, but Mabel doesn't buy it.

"I told you about my experience with long distance." Mabel dropped her gaze. "I don't want—"

Lisandra placed a hand on Mabel's cheek and gently raised her face so their eyes can meet.

"Don't think like that. I'm not Norma."

"I-I just don't know."

Mabel fell into Lisandra's arms, and they held one another in silence.

"Get a room," Graci jokes, as her and Xavi come back inside from their cigarette break.

Mabel and Lisandra released and Graci saw that their faces were glistening with tears.

"Is everything okay?"

"Mabel got the assistantship. Our baby is Ph.D. bound." Lisandra wipes away the evidence of her true feelings.

"Oh, my goddess." Graci walked to Mabel and clapped her on the back. "Well done, kid. I guess I'll need to find some other hottie to sling the drinks at Loverbar."

Lisandra and Graci left promptly after they finished their meal. Both had work early in the morning, and Mabel's shift wasn't done until ten. The rest of dinner service proved slow, just as Mabel predicted. Not because there weren't people in Old San Juan, they just weren't in the mood for Chinese/Japanese fusion, apparently.

"Let me take you out for a drink to celebrate," Xavi said.

"There isn't much to celebrate, but what the hell."

"Then we can drink our sorrows away together." Xavi takes Mabel's arm and ushers her out of the restaurant.

Their regular bar had the usual suspects lingering around. They were all fascinated by a bachelorette party with six very drunk females in stilettos and short, tight dresses. Sashes drooped from their bare, sweaty shoulders, and much to the delight of the bar's straight, male customers, their skirts rode up with every hip swivel and shoulder shake. Their favorite bartender, Ceviche, is on duty.

"*Wepa, mi gente,* my people, how is life treating you?" Ceviche's energy was contagious, and Mabel couldn't help but smile.

"Significantly worse than it was treating me last week, Ceviche." Mabel took a seat at the bar and gestured for Xavi to do the same.

"You're still breathing, right? God is good all the time, and all the time God is good." Ceviche smiled as he whipped up some grapefruit vodkas.

"I've never been partial to your god," Mabel made quotation marks with her hands. "But I suppose he can't be that bad if he made you." Mabel winked.

"You're too good to me, Mabelita." Ceviche served them the grapefruit vodkas.

One of the bachelorettes draped herself over the bar.

"B—bartender, a round of tequila shots, please." Emphasis on the 'ease.'

"Good luck with that mess." Xavi nodded toward the bachelorettes.

Ceviche winked and went on his way.

"Permission to speak about the assistantship?" Xavi asked as he took a sip of his drink.

Mable nodded and sipped her vodka grapefruit as well.

"What are you going to do?"

"I don't know."

"Just make sure you don't bail because you're scared."

Mabel took another swig of the drink. She appreciates that Ceviche went heavy on the vodka.

"If you stay for Lisandra, your family, your life, fine. I get it. But don't use that as an excuse to stay because you're scared. That's all I'm saying."

Mabel wanted to assure him that she wasn't scared, that staying is all about Lisandra and home, but she can't. She chugged her drink.

"I'm sorry, I shouldn't have—"

"No, it's okay." Mabel relaxed her shoulders and rolled her neck around. "*Tienes razón,* you're right."

Xavi rubbed her back and finished his drink. Both drinks were empty, and Ceviche was still dealing with the bachelorettes. The one draped on the bar suggestively rubbed his arm. Meanwhile, her friends giggled and not-so-subtlety whispered, "Get him, blowjob queen."

"I'll tell you who should be scared," Mabel gestured toward the shameless flirting at the other end of the bar. "Ceviche. That bitch is thirsty."

Ceviche looked at Mabel and Xavi with eyes that cry for help. They laughed and shrugged their shoulders.

"I'm going to pee, be right back."

Mabel got up and made her way up the spiral staircase that led to the second floor of the bar where the bathrooms and pool tables were housed. Carefully, she followed the steps up. Many a fool had slipped and busted their butt on these stairs, including Mabel. As the night progressed at the bar, the regulars always turned to watch when people went up and down the stairs. A resounding moan permeated the bar every time someone fell victim to the slippery stairs.

Mabel made it up without incident, which meant she was not nearly as tipsy as she wanted to be. So many potential tears on the horizon. Thinking about goodbyes made her stomach hurt. Luckily, there were not many people upstairs, the pool tables were empty, and there wasn't a line of ladies clenching their thighs desperate for a stall.

Sitting on the toilet, Mabel checked her phone. No messages. Lisandra must be asleep. She hoped she's okay and not reeling from the news. Mabel typed a message.

Don't you want me to stay?

Her finger hovered above the send button. Someone entered the bathroom with a loud stumble. It must be one of the blitzed bachelorettes. Mabel erased the message and finished up in the stall. It's the one that was hitting on Ceviche. The bachelorette attempted to fix her hair and make-up in front of the mirror. She swayed on her heels while digging through her purse. The purse fell, spilling the contents on the bathroom floor. Lipstick, condoms, powder, keys, gum, napkins.

"Crap," the bachelorette muttered, as she squatted down.

Unable to maintain her balance, she fell. Mabel hurried

to her and gathered the spilled contents of the purse. Then, she helped the bachelorette up.

"Thanks, you're really n—nice." The bachelorette hiccuped. "Most w—women are bitches to me."

"Maybe you're hanging with the wrong women."

The bachelorette is quiet for a second then laughed. "You're blunt. I bet women hate you, too."

Mable chuckled. "Not exactly."

The bachelorette steadied herself and extended a hand. "I'm Susana."

"Mabel."

They shook hands. Susana looked Mabel up and down.

"Did you g—get off work or something." She hiccuped. "Cuz this," she pointed at Mabel's outfit. "It doesn't read like going-out attire."

Mabel laughed and washed her hands.

"Looks like you're pretty blunt, too. I see why you have trouble with the ladies."

Susana frowned. "I'm sorry, that was so r—rude."

"No, it was honest. Is it you getting married?" Mabel tried to calm her curls which had been frizzed out by the humidity.

Susana guffawed, throwing her long, blonde hair back.

"Hell, no. Not my bag." Susana slurred her words. "What about you?" She pointed a wobbly finger at Mabel. "Do you have a special someone?"

"Yes, but I may have to leave her." The sadness from before remerged, first in her mind, then it spread and spread through her body like a virus.

"That sucks. Why?" Susana wiped at the mascara melting down her face.

"To get my Ph.D."

"Whoa. Soon-to-be Doctor Mabel. That's awesome."

"I don't know if I'm going."

"Oh." Susana messed with her crooked Bride Tribe sash.

Mabel sighed, looked at the floor, and prepared herself for the look of bewilderment and the encouragement not to let anything stand in the way of her dreams. Even strangers couldn't wait to tell her what was best.

"Let me guess. I'm crazy for not diving into this opportunity headfirst."

"Huh?" Susana looked up from her sash which was still crooked. "Oh, not really. I get it."

Mable looked at Susana, her eyebrows raised. "You do?"

"Sure." Susana stumbled toward Mabel. "People always try to tell me what to do. Don't do another shot, don't sleep with someone you just met, eat breakfast, ugh. It's like, shut up and let me be me, you know?"

Mabel nodded and readied herself in case Susana fell again. Susana placed a heavy hand on Mabel's shoulder and tried to make her face look serious.

"Listen," Susana hiccupped. "I'm going to give you some m—million-dollar advice."

Mabel leaned in, ready. Susana hiccupped again making Mabel jump. Susana laughed, Mabel rolled her eyes.

"Sorry, sorry. Okay, here it is for real." Susana got closer. "Do whatever you want."

Susana disengaged from Mabel, took another look in the mirror, finally managed to straighten her sash, and headed to the door. She stopped and turned before exiting.

"Look, it's easy. I want another shot." She hiccupped. "What does Dr. Mabel want?"

Susana exited the restroom, leaving Mabel in the same position by the mirror. Mabel looked at herself then took her phone out of her bag. She pulled up the acceptance letter and read the words again.

We're pleased to offer you a Teaching Assistantship for the 2019-2020 academic year —

Mabel smiled, put the phone back in her bag, and left. She made her way to that treacherous spiral staircase and begins her descent. Carefully, she takes it one step at a time. The regulars perched at the bar watch, wait for her to slip, but she doesn't. She made it all the way down without incident.

Mabel creeps up on Xavi who is waiting at the bar with two, new drinks. She taps his shoulder, making him jump.

"¡*Ay, santo*! Are you trying to give me a heart attack?" Xavi places a hand on his chest.

Mabel throws her head back and laughs, long and deep. A new sort of relaxed energy permeates her body. She sits down, grabs the new drink Xavi has waiting for her, and raises it like an offering to Ceviche's god.

"To doing whatever we want."

"I can get behind that." Xavi raises his glass. "To doing whatever we want."

"*Salud,* cheers," they say in unison, clink, and take a drink.

Chapter Nine

The Show Must Go On

"*Ay, Señor. Me voy a reventar*, I'm going to explode."

"Abuela Aida, just stop eating fried shit."

"Lola, language." Lola's mother turns from the cutting board where she is mincing onions and points the blade at Lola.

Lola rolls her eyes. Meanwhile, Abuela Aida massages her bloated belly.

"This is *not* because of food. Ese doctor has no idea what he's talking about. I'm too old and I've been through too much to not eat whatever the hell I want."

"Whatever you say, Mom." Lola's mother shakes her head. "Lola, add Pepto to the grocery list."

Lola writes Pepto at the bottom of the list and includes the price. She frowns. The list is more than the allotted items the family had agreed upon to remain within budget. She doesn't know why they bother with a list.

Just last week, Lola had to dip into her savings to cover groceries, savings meant to be used to fix up the family car. The air conditioner, speakers, right taillight, left blinker, and windshield wipers are busted. The car will not pass inspection next time they have to renew their registration if repairs are not made, and that car is the family's only means of transportation. It got Lola's mother to her job at Marshalls, now suspended because of the pandemic, Lola's Abuela Aida to her doctor's appointments, and Lola to the performances that helped keep the family financially afloat. Not that there are any performances happening now thanks to COVID. Twenty twenty can suck it.

Lola's mother notices the expression on her daughter's face.

"Marshall's will open back up soon. This won't last, you'll see." Lola's mother strokes her daughter's face.

Lola places her hand on her mother's and breathes in her scent. The familiar smell relaxed Lola's shoulders which always creep up to her ears when she's thinking about money.

"I know, *Mami.*"

"And when they reopen, I'm up for a promotion and you won't have to be out at all hours of the night." She kisses Lola on the forehead and goes back to mincing.

Lola sighs.

"Mom, you know I'm not out there just partying. Performing is my job, I love it, and I love that it helps pay the bills."

"I just don't understand why you have to be so crude when you perform. People could get the wrong idea, assume things about you, about our family."

Lola's stomach turns.

"What are you talking about? Assume what? It's performance with a purpose, Mami. It's about freedom of expression, opposing bullshit societal expectations."

"Language." Her mother points the blade at Lola again.

Placing the knife down, she takes a breath then turns to face her daughter.

"*No estoy de acuerdo*, Lola. It's just not right, strutting around on stage practically naked to that awful music. Drugs, sex, drinking. What will people at church say if they find out?"

"I don't give a shit."

Her mother takes hold of the knife and recommences mincing. The striking of the knife on the cutting board grows louder. Lola opens her mouth to speak but decides not to.

Lola looks at the kitchen counter where the bills are beginning to pile up again. They had disappeared completely a month before the pandemic hit thanks to Lola's performances. Before COVID struck hard, Lola was making more than she ever had with her gigs, and it was all thanks to her raunchy, fashion pig persona. The hyper-feminine, polished pageant queen aesthetic wasn't for her, and audiences loved her for it. Now, if only her mother would, too. Lola stands from the kitchen table and makes her way to her room. Abuela Aida reaches out and takes her arm as she walks by.

"It'll be fine, *m'ija*, you'll see." Abuela Aida strokes her granddaughter's arm. "Now, go get my Pepto before I die."

The line at the grocery store spills out into the parking lot.

Lola, being the youngest and thus most protected against sickness in the family, is tasked with retrieving the family's groceries until the stores get their delivery and pick-up services running smoothly. Lola struggles to put on the makeshift mask her mother made from an old T-shirt using a tutorial she saw on Mega TV. She waits in line scrolling through her phone for job openings. No one is hiring.

She ceases the job search and turns to her bank account. There's barely enough for today's groceries. She is going to need to figure something out if she wants to keep her family fed and medicated. Her phone goes off.

"*Hola, nena.* What's up?" It's Xavier.

Lola and Xavier grew up together. He knew Lola before her transformation, and Lola knew him when he was a closet *cuir* memorizing the choreography to Britney Spears' "Hit Me Baby One More Time."

"Baby! *¿Cómo estás?* The crew misses you. Do you want to video chat with me, Pinky, Valeria, Graci, and Alan tonight? We are going to watch Landon Cider's live show on Instagram—full transformation, performance, Q&A, the works, should be fun."

Lola smiled, embracing the warmth of Xavier's voice.

"I wish I could, but unless Graci is planning on opening Loverbar soon, I have to focus on finding some kind of job."

"She would if she could, but COVID is a bitch. The quarantine is holding-up licensing and keeping Loverbar from opening. If you feel like taking a break, you know where to find us. Virtual drag party."

Lola perks up at Xavier's words. Why didn't she think of it before?

"Xavi, you're a freakin' genius. I'm going to have to call you back."

Lola spends the rest of her time in line working that executive realness, sending texts, and making calls to set up her very own virtual drag show. Graci, Alan, Pinky, and Valeria promise to do everything they can to promote the event and create hype but there's still one problem. Lola is technologically impaired and will require some help.

Lola searches through her contacts until she finds the perfect person. She shoots him a text.

Mi amor, how are you? I need a pro-bono favor, nothing fancy, just a simple flyer, something flashy I can post to Insta and Facebook.

"Lola. Of course, anything for my favorite queen. I miss going to your shows."

"That's actually exactly what this favor is about."

Two days later, Lola studies the flyer for her virtual drag show. Large lettering.

La Famosa Fashion Lola's Insta Live Extravaganza-Sunday @8pm on Insta Live

The words are on a hot pink background trimmed in a gold confetti pattern. Lola's most flattering headshot sits next to the lettering. She smiled.

Lola opens Instagram and attempts to upload the promo flyer.

Couldn't refresh feed. No network connection.

Lola tries again.

Couldn't refresh feed. No network connection.

"*Sea la madre*, damn it!" She pops her head out of her room. "Mami, do you have Internet on your phone?"

"No. And I'm out of data, too."

Lola made her way to the modem, and it's as expected. No blinking lights, no connection. Then, the house goes dark and silent sending Lola's heart into her stomach. The power is out. The lack of noise is unbearable any time the constant hum of the fan, which is always on, stops.

Tierra trágame, this isn't happening. "I wish the Earth would swallow me whole," Lola repeats in mumble.

Lola's face grows hot, and her leg begins to bounce. No solutions come to mind. The one electric company that services the entire island always has issues. Blackouts are a daily occurrence, and Lola can't go out to find power and wi-fi, COVID has made sure of that. She lays back in bed and covers her face with her hands. Her breath quickens, as she wonders how long she can stay under the covers without being bothered, hiding from reality as she did from monsters. She focuses on lengthening her breath, and after a few cycles, she uncovers her face.

With nothing she can do for her virtual show, Lola turns to cleaning the house.

"Wow, *y esto*? Who did this?" Abuela Aida surfaces from her room and stares at the living room and kitchen.

Lola is scrubbing the sink.

"Me, *obvio*, I *do* know how to clean."

"Now, I know. This, I've never seen. What you did before today hardly qualifies as cleaning," Abuela Aida says, making air quotes.

Lola rolls her eyes and keeps scrubbing. Abuela Aida tries to sneak a bag of chips from the pantry, but Lola knows her play and turns and blocks her right as she is about to make her getaway. Lola takes the chips and replaces them with a bag of shredded carrots. Abuela Aida scrunches up her face, places the bag on the kitchen counter, and tries to storm off but only manages a slight shuffle thanks to the arthritis in her joints. Abuela Aida stops and turns to Lola.

"Everything looks great. Well done, *m'ija*." Abuela Aida winks before disappearing into the hallway.

Lola smiles and keeps scrubbing while occasionally glancing at the modem. It's still not illuminated. Lola cleans and stares, cleans and stares. She finishes scrubbing and dries off the sink. One more look.

Five hours later, the promo is picking up on social media. Forty likes so far and a few comments of encouragement. This is a good start, but not enough. At least the promo has all day tomorrow to gain more traction. Lola abandons the phone and turns her attention to the closet. Somewhere in that dark abyss lies her performance banner. The closet is a maze of clothing, products, and shoes. She sifts and removes, digs and digs. After fifteen minutes of this, a familiar bit of pink glossy material peeks out from beneath some shoe boxes. She unearths the banner and unfolds it, smiling.

She had it made three months before COVID hit. Xavier thought it would give her a greater sense of legitimacy. Plus, numbers don't lie, and every show in which she used the banner featuring her trademark fashion pig resulted in a spike of Instagram followers and YouTube views. #ILoveLolalLove.

"*Viste*, if you would listen to me more often, you would've already made it big by now," Xavier said after Lola's first show featuring the banner.

Lola rolled her eyes but smirked. I hate to admit it, but

maybe you're right."

Xavier became her unofficial manager after that. She consulted him anytime she needed practical advice about her gigs, which is what she needs now. Lola furrows her brow as she thinks of ways to monetize the virtual drag show. Nothing. If she doesn't figure this out, Abuela will be without meds. Lola's eyes turn glassy. She shakes her head and rubs her eyes. Plus, the bills and groceries. More tears threaten to emerge, but Lola gets Xavier on the phone before they can.

"Hey, love. *¿Cómo estás?*"

"Ay, ma'. You know how it goes, just hustling trying to help Angel with his desserts and deliveries. Since the restaurant shut down, I have to do what I can to help with our cash flow problems."

"That's actually what I'm calling about. I have an idea that could make us some money."

"You had me at money."

"Virtual drag show. If Landon Cider can do it, why can't we? All we need is a virtual tip jar, a way people can donate."

"Yes, yes, yes. Don't worry, I got you on the virtual tip jar. Links to your PayPal and ATH Mobile. That way we accommodate people who don't have Banco Popular. Can you say international audience, baby?"

"Xavi, you're my hero. I'll text you what time to arrive tomorrow.

"I'll be there."

The next morning, Lola's mother pokes her head into Lola's room.

"*Levántate*, it's time to wake."

Lola is busy making her bed which is no longer buried under a thick layer of her things. Her mother looks around wide-eyed.

"You're up early, and you cleaned. What's the occasion?"

"I'm going to try to work from home." Lola fluffs her pillows.

Her mother furrows her brow.

"What kind of work is it that you're going to do?"

Lola turns to face her mother, narrowing her eyes. "Are you asking if I'm doing something you don't approve of?"

She retrieves the banner from beneath her bed and begins smoothing it out.

Her mother drops her gaze and sighs.

"*Me decepcionas*, Lola. You disappoint me." Her mother leaves the room.

Lola stands up, makes her way to the door, and slams it. She turns to face the banner smoothed out on the floor and falls back against the door. She closes her eyes and slowly slides down the door until she is on the floor. She takes deep breaths willing away the thoughts making her want to scream and smash shit up. Lola balls and releases her fists repeatedly. A soft knock gets her attention.

"Lola, are you okay, *m'ija*? I overheard—"

"Si, Abuela. It's just...allergies."

"Bueno, whatever you're planning, I'm sure it will work out."

Lola does not respond.

After her room is all set, she makes one last call to Xavier.

"Come around nine."

"Is your mom cool with this?"

"No. Apparently, I'm a disappointment. But she can't stop me. We need the money."

"Ay, baby."

"It's fine, I'm used to it. Come in through my window, if I tell her you're coming to help me with this, she'll lose her shit."

Lola starts getting ready around seven thirty. She decides to emphasize her eyes with silver by expertly recreating the effect of a delicate shimmering mask with eyeshadow and glitter. Thick, cat-eye style black liquid liner follows along with a pair of faux lashes. She paints her lips with a black matte lipstick. Instead of her usual blowout, Lola goes with curls making sure to use the extra-hold mousse. Last, she wraps herself in a pink robe.

Lola squirms as she remembers the post-show pictures where she looked more wet dog than diva. She grabs the hairspray, gives her do a once over, and finds herself in the mirror. Lola studies the look she created. She narrows her eyes, intensifying her gaze. A seductive smile stretches across her face. A knock at the door brings humility back to Lola's face. Her mother speaks from behind the door.

"I'm going to bed. *Buenas noches.* Try not to keep me up with your racket."

Lola closes her eyes and takes a breath.

"*Buenas noches, Mami.*" Lola looks at the door, but it doesn't open.

She hears soft footsteps fading away.

Lola finds herself in the mirror once more.

Let's do this.

The banner is alive with the cascading colors of the LED lights Lola purchased at Marshall's with her mother's discount. Blue turns to green to yellow to orange and so on down the color spectrum. Lola looks at the time on her phone. No messages. Her hands are trembling. She shakes them shooing away the negative energy. She checks the promo flyer on Instagram, the amount of likes and comments suggest the following she worked so hard to accrue before the pandemic is eager to see her in action again.

A pebble hits the window.

Lola jumps, letting out a squeal. She cautiously approaches the window and slowly peers out. Xavier is a foot or so below waving his hands.

"You scared the shit out of me."

"*Mala mía,* but you try getting here so close to that stupid curfew. I had to straight ninja this shit." Xavier extends his arms reaching for Lola.

After a few failed attempts, Lola pulls him into her room.

"Everything is set up, including the info for virtual tips. We got ATH mobile, PayPal, and I've also included Venmo."

"I told you once, and I'll tell you again, you're a freakin' genius."

"I have my moments." Xavi dusts his shoulders off. "*Lista?*"

"Ready."

Xavier starts the live and motions her to begin with a point.

"Welcome, darlings, to the first-ever Lola Insta Live Extravaganza." Lola waves her hands in front of her face like a magician mid-illusion. "I have some songs and mixes I want to perform for you, *pero* I'm also *puesta p'al* request, ready to take some requests. So, grab a drinkie-poo, sit back, and enjoy. And if you like what you see, help a sistah out and show me some love in the virtual tip jar. Times are tough everywhere thanks to that ho, COVID, so, anything you donate will be much appreciated. It all goes directly to the Lola Love foundation for feeding and taking care of Abuela Aida and mother."

Lola gives her back to the camera and looks over her shoulder.

"Let's get this party started."

"Venus" by Lady Gaga starts and Lola turns to face the camera. Slowly, she undoes the robe and reveals a black corset, pink crop top, pink thigh-high platform boots, and a silver mini skirt with a prosthetic penis prominently strapped to it. She walks toward the camera modeling and posing with every step as she lip-syncs. She can feel the familiar tingle of adrenaline coursing through her agile body. High kick, turn, vogue, high kick, her movements are sharp, hitting every beat. Lady Gaga sings.

Lola sensually slides her hands down between her breasts and over her stomach until taking hold of the prosthetic penis and giving it a hard shake, which culminates in an energetic hip thrust. As the song winds down, Lola goes into a death drop, back rolls, jumps into the air, and lands in a split to conclude the number.

Xavier smiles and bounces silently giving Lola frantic thumbs-ups. Viewers must be reacting well.

"*Gracias todes*, thank you all. Make sure to share the live, tell your friends, your girl, your guy, your person, the more the merrier."

The virtual drag show continues for an hour and a half with Lola performing her classics as well as viewer requests.

After the live, Lola collapses into her bed.

"I'm so proud of you, baby." Xavier sits next to her on the bed.

"If only my mom was," Lola says, her eyes closed.

"Mind if I crash here? I'll skip out first thing in the morning."

"Of course, baby. Thank you for everything."

Lola wakes to knocking on her door. Lola rubs her eyes and yawns. She looks in the mirror and sees she's still wearing last night's look. Xavier already left.

"Come in."

Abuela Aida pokes her head into the room. "*Buenos días, m'ija.*"

"Good morning, Abuela."

"How did it go? The music kept me up all night."

"I'm sorry, Abuela."

"You won't have to be if you made us some *dinerito.*"

Lola realizes she has not checked how much she made last night.

"Your mother went to church. She seemed upset."

Lola sighs and rubs her neck.

"I'll talk to her when she gets home."

The wait for her mother seems to drag on and on as Lola imagines her mother scolding her. She focuses on cleaning up her room which is spotless when her mother arrives.

"*Hola*, Mami, how was church?"

"It was fine." Her mother does not make eye contact. "You should come with me sometime."

Lola contains the urge to say, as if I'm welcome there, and decides instead to change the subject.

"I think the show went well. I'm about to check how much I made."

Her mother silently puts up her purse.

"You know, you could at least pretend to care. I don't know why I even bother." Lola begins walking away, wishing the pandemic was past and she could walk out the front door.

"Lola, *por favor*. Come here."

"Look, Mom, if this is going to be another guilt trip, I'd rather skip to the part where I disappoint you so I can leave."

Lola's mother sighs, her gaze meeting Lola's. Her mother made her way to the couch, sits, and motions for Lola to join her. Lola does not comply at first, but soon relents and sits by her mother, her heart palpitating. Here it comes.

"I couldn't sleep last night."

Lola rolls her eyes.

"Mom, it's the only way I can make money in this fuck—"

Lola catches herself. "In this pandemic."

"Not because of the music, because of what I said to you."

Lola's eyes widen.

"I was at your door. I knew Xavier was here. I heard what you said about taking care of me and Abuela. My not agreeing with how you express yourself is no excuse for what I said to you."

Lola sits still, her hands tucked between her thighs. Yelling she was ready for, but this?

"*No me decepcionas.* Without you during all of this, I don't know how me and your Abuela would've—" Her mother's lower lip trembles until the tears can't be contained.

Lola looks at her mother, sighs, and puts an arm around her.

"*Mami,* it's okay."

"Please, let me finish." Her mother takes a few breaths. "I-I just," she sighs heavily. "Thank you."

Lola can feel pressure in her throat, as she tries to contain her tears.

"I still don't agree with you being vulgar."

Lola removes her arm from around her mother.

"But how you express yourself is your business, especially if it's making us money."

Remembering she has yet to verify her earnings, Lola grabs her phone and logs into her various accounts.

"Lola, please, put your phone down. I'm trying to talk to you."

Ignoring her mother, Lola's eyes widen as she takes in her earnings. Smirking, she raises the phone to her mother's face.

"Are you cool with me being vulgar now?"

Chapter Ten

Casi

The bar looks better than Graci had ever imagined. She spent the day finalizing the décor. A combination of hot pink walls peppered with vintage records, neon-colored stools, a small but sufficient stage for performances, fun and fuzzy furniture that was every female millennial tween's dream, and a community closet that screamed thrift-store chic. All she has to do is drop off the rent and the safe space for all will be ready to open next month.

Graci looks down at her Wonder Woman watch. Seeing that it's nine, she decides to call it a day and head home. Cops are being real jerks about the ten o'clock curfew. Not that it matters, she has to wake up early to drop the rent off anyway. Being the first at the office will ensure that she is able to leave before noon. If she gets there after they have already opened, she's in for hours of tortured waiting while the employees take their time sipping coffee, answering personal calls, and dragging their feet to and from the bathroom.

Graci takes one final look at the bar, smiles, shuts the door, and locks it. Three years and a parade of setbacks later, she can finally see the finish line. Loverbar will be ready to open as soon as Graci and her employees test out the food and drink menus.

The streets of Rio Piedras are empty, void of the young and restless that used to roam its streets before COVID established curfews. She wouldn't be able to stay open late or function at full capacity for a while, but she didn't care. She just wants to get the business going so that when the curfew and masks are history, Loverbar is in solid shape and ready to accept all the island's *cuir* children.

On her way home, Graci spots her favorite piece of street art, an image of Antoine de Saint-Exupéry's *The Little Prince* with the message *Lo esencial es invisible para el gobierno* next to it. What is essential is invisible to the government. She stops to admire it for a second but is distracted when she hears a faint sound behind her. Graci looks around but does not see anything. It was probably the wind scattering some trash. Goosebumps emerge on the back of Graci's neck sending a chill through her body despite the eighty-five-degree heat. Graci decides to cut her viewing short and picks up the pace toward her apartment. She dreads the parts of the sidewalk that are not illuminated by lampposts. The electric grid is still not reconstructed, and shoddy wiring, poles, and towers are still prevalent on the island.

Graci hears something again, this time it's consistent and growing louder, footsteps. Her heart pounds as she debates whether to run, turn around, or do nothing. The choice is made for her when she feels something shove into her back.

"*La cartera, ahora, rápido.* The purse, now, quickly." The gunman pushes Graci into a wall.

Graci is trembling, scouring her mind for a way to get out of this. The rent is in her purse, and she can't afford to let this loser take it.

"*P-por favor—*"

The gunman pushes the gun farther into Graci's back.

"*Cállate.* Shut up. *Cartera, ahora. Y el reloj también.*" Great, Graci thinks when he demands her watch too. Is the gunman thorough or just greedy?

"No. Please, not my watch. I-It's not worth anything."

"*¡Ahora!*" The gunman pushes harder.

Graci winces at the object digging into her back. She sees her Wonder Woman watch and wishes she was more like the warrior princess. But she's no Amazon. Graci lets the purse slide out of her hand onto the ground, unbuckles the watch, and drops it too. She hears shuffling as the gunman retrieves the objects, all the while his gun firmly planted against the back of Graci's spine. Now that he has what he wants, at least he'll be gone soon.

The moment extends as the gunman remains behind Graci. Why isn't he leaving? She feels a hand touch her hip and slide down her leg. Afraid to set off the gun, Graci remains paralyzed. The hand continues trailing along her skin making its way under Graci's skirt. The urge to scream builds and builds, but Graci resists. She feels the hand slide between her thighs, the urge can no longer be contained.

"¡*No me toques*! Don't touch me." Graci falls to the ground and covers her head.

She remains on the ground shaking, waiting for the gunman to retaliate. When nothing happens, Graci opens her eyes and looks around. The gunman is gone. Graci is a shivering mess practically laying on the concrete. The smell of old, rancid urine fills her nostrils. Fucking filthy streets. Even after all this time, after the hurricane, after quarantine, it still smells like piss.

The next thing she knows, Graci is standing in front of her elderly neighbor's door, not recalling the walk there. Graci had given her neighbor a spare key to the apartment about a year ago. Even sober, Graci manages to lose her keys and lock herself out all the time. This is exactly what she tells the neighbor happened when the elderly woman asks, since Graci does not want to worry her. She considers calling the police and filing a report, but what good would that do? That asshole is long gone by now.

Graci sits on her futon, a cigarette clutched between her right index and middle fingers. Her hand shakes, making the smoke rise in a jagged and uneven manner. Usually, she enjoys trying to create smooth, streams of smoke, but nothing seems to be able to soothe her.

I know what will soothe you—

Not this again. It has been a while since Karen spoke up in Graci's head. Of course, staying sober has been hard as hell but moments like this when Karen is extra loud are the worst. The desire is always there, but when something terrible happens, that desire is heightened. Graci can still feel the ghost of the gunman's hand sliding up her skirt. It makes her shake so violently she drops the cigarette.

"Crap. Crap!" Graci flicks it off the futon and onto the tiled floor where she safely stomps it out.

She paces to ignore the itch that is spreading across her body. Long inhale, long exhale, long inhale, long exhale. Just return to the breath, just return to the breath. But she can still feel the gunman. And the money. Shit, the money.

All you need is something that will take the edge off—

"Oh, my god. At least he didn't hurt you." Alan hugs Graci.

She failed to include the part about the wandering hand when recounting last night's events. She's managed to stop shaking since then, but the cigarette smoking has not ceased.

"What about the money? How am I going to pay the bar's rent now?" She takes a long drag from the cigarette in her hand and blows it out. "I can't have anything delay this opening."

Graci looks around at the fully decorated bar and feels her stomach turn. They were so close.

"It's going to be fine." Alan places a hand on Graci's shoulder.

She stands up knocking Alan's hand off.

"Valeria, Pinky, Lola, and Sammy are relying on the jobs I offered them here."

"Our friends will understand. It's not your fault that jackhole robbed you."

"Yeah, but I let him take the money." Graci takes another puff of the cigarette.

"Let? Are you insane? He could've killed you."

Graci wishes he would've. She taps her cigarette on the Liza Minnelli ashtray sitting on the table and sits back down.

"Whatever, it doesn't matter now. Lola and the others will be here any minute for the tasting."

Alan's brow is furrowed as he listens.

"Are you sure you're okay?"

"I'm fine." Graci forces a smile.

The hand holding the cigarette is shaking, but she lowers it under the table before Alan can notice.

Lola and Xavier are the first to arrive. They greet Graci and Alan giving them each a kiss on the cheek and a hug.

"I see those virtual drag shows are killing." Graci has tuned into every show so far.

"Yes, mamma. If it weren't for that little hustle, ya' girl would be on the streets suckin' dick and turnin' tricks for a little bit of paper."

Graci laughs.

"Thanks for all the tips, by the way." Lola winks at Graci. "How are you?"

Graci remembers the feeling of the gun digging deeper and deeper into her back. She feels her heart palpitate at an incredible speed. She doesn't want to remember what came next. Victimized by that stupid sexist hand.

"I'm great, just ready to open this place up. Why don't we start getting the bar and kitchen ready so we can get to cooking, mixing, and tasting when the rest of the crew arrives?"

Xavier and Lola get right on it. Alan remains.

"Aren't you going to tell them?"

"No, this stays between us. I don't want anyone to worry about the opening getting delayed any further, or about me. I'll figure it out."

"Okay, it's your story to tell." Alan follows Lola and Xavier into the kitchen.

When Valeria, Pinky, and Sammy arrive, the crew gets to work preparing the items on the drink and food menus. They finish cooking and mixing and lay the drinks and dishes on the bar top. The Femmebot Pinka-colada looks particularly appetizing to Graci who can't help but linger on the mixed drink while taking in the spread. Of course, she will only sample the food. Alan oversees making the final decision on drinks. All the food is delicious, but the veggie burger is Graci's favorite with its crispy lettuce, three cheeses, and cilantro lime aioli. A nice, cold beer would go perfectly with it. Maybe they should have a beer and veggie burger special. Alan prefers the fruity waffle which they will offer during brunch, perfect with a mimosa.

When the crew turns to sipping and tasting the drinks, Graci focuses on cleaning up the food. She gathers as many plates as she can and makes for the kitchen hoping the distance between her and the booze will stop the itch that keeps growing and growing, spreading. Graci drops the dishes in the kitchen sink and begins scrubbing away.

Long inhale, equally long exhale. Just focus on the breath.

"Ow." Graci yanks her hand out of the soapy water, her finger bleeding.

One of the plates must've broken when she dropped them in. It's a microscopic cut, but blood is already emerging, a perfect little ruby. Graci sticks her finger in her mouth and sucks. She closes her eyes and refocuses on breathing.

"You okay in there?" Alan's voice carries into the kitchen.

"I'm fine, just a little cut."

Graci finishes cleaning the rest of the dishes trying to block out the crew's conversations which get progressively gigglier as the tasting continues. When she's done with the dishes, she turns her attention to the entire kitchen which is impeccable by the time Alan calls out again.

"Graci, we are all done up here."

Alan and Lola stay behind to help with the cleanup. Alan rinses most of the glasses and containers that have alcohol in them. Most of them. He misses a little plastic cup with excess Femmebot Pinka-colada that is well hidden by the grenadine. Graci notices but says nothing.

When he's done, Alan takes out the trash.

"Any other trash left?" Alan is standing at the back exit that leads to the dumpster.

"Nope. Oh, please make sure you separate the recycling," Graci says, eyeing the Grenadine hiding the Pinka-colada.

"Ugh, I forgot about that. On it."

Alan exits through the back leaving Lola and Graci to clean the bar top. Lola's phone rings.

"I'll be right back, it's Mom." Lola makes a finger gun and shoots herself in the head. Graci nods, and Lola exits through the front of the bar. Graci is left alone. Her hands start to shake. She looks down at them and notices just how naked her left wrist feels without her Wonder Woman watch.

A little bit of that would still the nerves.

"No, no, no, Karen. Abso-fuckin-lutely not." Graci reaches for a cigarette, her hand trembling.

The carton in her purse is empty.

"Crap." Graci paces while the assault plays again and again in her head.

Without the rent, the opening will be pushed back. You could get kicked out, or the landlord could jack up the price. There's no way of getting the money in time. Now, you risk leaving your friends jobless for who knows how long. They were all counting on you, and you messed up.

Graci shakes her head trying to shake Karen. She can hear Lola yelling at her mother outside and tries to focus on

the shouting. Trying to make out the conversation might distract her from how velvety smooth the Pinka-colada looks.
No matter how hard she tries, Graci can't pull away from that
small plastic cup. It pulls and pulls her in, the water receding,
sucking Graci into the massive wave of temptation that will
inevitably come crashing down in three, two, one—

Chapter Eleven

Epilogue

"We're almost at capacity." Alan has to shout for Graci to hear him as he admits people into the bar.

"Already?" Graci looks around at the crowd.

It's not even ten and the bar is packed. Thank goddess curfews are a thing of the past. COVID still lingers even though it's been two years since the initial quarantine, but at least the bar can stay open late. The five-dollar cover is going to go a long way in getting the performers paid. It's nice to finally see faces uncovered. For a while there, it seemed the masks would never come off. All the tables are taken. Groups chat and laugh while feasting on drinks, appetizers, and entrees. No faces of concern or anxiety scoping the bar, just relaxed bodies bonding with their buddies. Graci smiled.

"Is Lola ready to go?" Alan raises an eyebrow.

"Well—" Graci feigns concern.

Alan rolls his eyes and sighs.

"I'm just kidding. *Tranquilo*, you know Lola hasn't started a show late since Xavi officially became her manager." Graci shoves Alan's shoulder playfully.

Alan clutches his chest. "*Ay, nena*! Don't do that to me."

Alan refocuses on his role as the official doorman for the evening. He always takes care of the door for Graci when there is a drag event.

"Hey, beautiful."

Graci and Alan turn to find Bea, Graci's girlfriend, standing behind them. They've been together a few months now.

"They need you at the bar."

"Okay, but first." Graci kisses Bea.

"You two are so adorable, I'm going to gag." Alan sticks his tongue out at the girls.

"We love you too, babes." Graci winks at Alan and heads to the bar where Valeria and Pinky are mixing drinks.

"Well? Will the coveted Valeria have a gentleman caller cruising by the bar tonight for a little bit of love?" Pinky sensually caresses the pestle she's using to mash mint leaves behind the bar.

Valeria laughs while opening a bottle of rum.

"No, no boys for me tonight. I've decided to take a bit of a break, focus on me for a bit. Self-care and all that shit. Graci swears by it. Speaking of our fearless leader, here she comes."

Graci smiles at their exchange. "What's up, ladies?"

"We need help restarting the POS system," Pinky says.

Graci notes the frozen screen and gets to work.

"Oh, and we are running out of ice and Medalla." Valeria lines up three cups and expertly fills them with the rum she just opened.

"Okay, I'll ask Bea to grab some. Anything else?"

"Oh, orange juice, we need more orange juice," Pinky says, mixing a mojito.

As Graci walks out from behind the bar, Lola, the master of the evening's ceremony, walks out on stage. Lola's hips swivel smoothly from side to side as she model-walks her way center stage where there's a banner *Drab to Fab: Celebrating the Drag Journey.*

"*Buenas noches, corille!*"

The crowd claps and cheers, occasionally screaming. "Lola, *te amo!*"

"We have a fabulous lineup of queens, kings, and other incredible non-binary performers for y'all's delectation this evening, starting with yours truly," Lola raises her hands in the air presenting herself. "La Fashion Lola de San Juan motherfucking Puerto Ricooooooo."

The crowd hoots and hollers, throwing up the occasional whistle.

"Many of us have come a long way to be here and others still have a long way to go, so make sure you keep them tips comin', honey." Lola rubs her thumb and index fingers together. "Okay. Enough with the pleasantries, let's get dirty. DJ play my shit."

The Spanish ensemble song, "Resistiré 2020", erupts from the speakers. Lola begins strutting, gyrating, and sexually gesturing at individuals in the crowd. Graci whistles and hoots, catching Lola's eye. Lola dances her way to Graci and ushers her to join her on stage. Graci shakes her head and backs up mouthing, no, no, no, I'm good. Lola winks at Graci and turns back to the crowd eagerly gathered around the stage waving dollar bills for her to collect.

As Lola performs, Graci makes her way around the floor asking people how they are enjoying the menu.

"Incredible!"

"*Todo delicioso.* Everything is delicious."

Graci gobbles up the rave reviews, growing taller with each compliment. By the time she gets to Robertito's table, she's all smiles.

"*Gracias por venir.*" Graci greets him with a kiss on the cheek.

"This place is amazing. Very impressive."

"Thanks, Rob. And thanks for posting about the bar online, it was a huge help."

"Don't mention it."

"And now, one of our new kings, our very own disco daddy—"

Graci and Robertito turn their attention to Lola on stage.

"Sammy Slayer!"

Sammy walks out on-stage wearing silver platform boots, lime green bellbottoms, and a bedazzled, white button-down. The music starts and Sammy goes full Travolta, lip-syncing to the Bee Gees as he points, steps, and hustles to the beat. Graci squeezes Robertito on the shoulder, says a silent good-bye. She makes her way to the bar's entrance and runs into Mabel and Lisandra. Graci hasn't seen Mabel since she left for school back in twenty nineteen, although she's kept tabs on her through Lisandra. The fact that they were making it work long distance proves how perfect they are together.

"Hey. I'm so glad you made it. How's school?"

"Exhausting, but I love it." Mabel smiled.

"I'm so happy for you." Graci squeezes Mabel's shoulder.

"And we're happy for you. This place looks amazing." Lisandra gestures around the bar.

"I'm going out for a smoke, but I'll come sit with you in a minute. We can chat and catch up."

"Sounds good." Mabel and Lisandra walk off holding

hands.

Graci leans against the wall outside of Loverbar and lit a cigarette. She takes a deep inhale, looks up at the sky, and slowly releases the smoke through her burgundy lips. Although the light pollution from the city hides the stars, Graci takes comfort knowing they're up there. The cigarette is static in her hand, a straight stream of smoke drifting higher and higher up as she smiles at the sky. Graci can hear the audience clapping and cheering inside and closes her eyes reveling in the sound.

"Hey, did you talk to Bea yet? We need that ice." Alan is standing at the doorway.

"Nope, but I'm on it."

Graci quickly finishes her cigarette, puts it out, and tosses it in a nearby trashcan. She looks around satisfactorily noting the cleanliness of the surrounding area.

"Hey, Alan. Sniff the air."

"What?"

"What does it smell like?"

Alan takes a big whiff of the air surrounding the bar.

"I don't smell anything."

"Exactly, the one bar in town that doesn't smell like piss. Quite the accomplishment."

Alan laughs.

"So, we bougie now?" Alan flips his invisible hair.

"Us?" Graci smiles. "Never."

Author's Note

Setting the Scene

On July 22, 2019, more than a million Puerto Ricans marched demanding the resignation of ex-governor Roselló. This was the first protest of its kind and of this magnitude in recent Puerto Rican history. Late July 24, 2019, Roselló commenced his resignation speech which ended exactly at the stroke of midnight amidst the Perreo Combativo en la Fortaleza movement where hundreds of Puerto Ricans gathered to bump and grind in protest of the deceitful administration. While many participated in this movement, the LGBTQIA+ community's leadership and involvement were particularly influential. This collection of short stories looks at how the Puerto Rican LGBTQIA+ community—referred to as the *cuir* community, to honor the term used by the LGTQIA+ community in Puerto Rico—revolted and led the charge against decades of unjust government.

The fictional stories that compose this collection are based on interviews conducted with members of the Puerto Rican *cuir* community— Adi Love, Jhoni Jackson (owner of the real Loverbar once located in Rio Piedras, Puerto Rico), Victoria Alejandra Cepeda, and Sebastián Hernández. The stories intend to show how the Puerto Rican LGBTQIA+ community used performative protest strategies such as drag performance and dance in 2019 in order to criticize the Puerto Rican administration, mobilize the masses, and dethrone a corrupt and unethical governor who scoffed at the deaths resulting from Hurricane María, expressed homophobic and misogynistic sentiments, and admitted to corruption. Additionally, the stories here address significant issues that affect the Puerto Rican *cuir* community, such as addiction, transphobic hate crimes, the COVID-19 pandemic, and societal acceptance.

Because the goal of my work is to bring attention to the *cuir* Puerto Rican experience and argue for the rights of queers of color as well as progressive change in Puerto Rico, I have provided a brief introduction that will help you fully understand the narratives and enhance the reading experience. This contextualizes the stories that follow by providing a brief history of U.S. relations with Puerto Rico, a discussion of how performance can function as protest, and an exploration of José Esteban Muñoz's theory of disidentification as it relates to Puerto Rican *cuir* and drag culture. Armed with this background knowledge, I hope you enjoyed the stories and walk away with a better understanding of both the general and *cuir* Puerto Rican experience.

On Puerto Rico/U.S. Relations

After Hurricane María passed in 2017, it was impossible to reach anyone on the island. The island's already outdated and faulty electrical grid was obliterated, and its cell phone towers destroyed. The news footage during and after the storm was horrifying. It would be days, even weeks, before many heard from loved ones. Additionally, islanders were without running water and power for months, and some places still, at the time of this writing, haven't fully recovered.

The U.S. administration responded in a sluggish manner, confirming Puerto Rico's continued colonial status and second-class citizenship. Despite the island's history with hurricanes, the U.S. administration failed to deploy the appropriate assistance in a timely manner, which resulted in an increased death-count and the people taking post-María recovery into their own hands.

The apathy with which Puerto Rico was treated during the aftermath of Hurricane María is proof that even though coloniality as an official system is technically gone, Puerto Rico's relationship to the United States is still one of coloniality where Puerto Ricans are treated as second-class citizens. The paradox is painfully evident. Puerto Ricans on the island are expected to abide by the laws, policies, and constitutional system of the U.S. Federal Government, but how can they when they are mistreated and not supported in return?

It all started when the U.S. took possession of the island in 1898. The colonial process began, and Puerto Rico was primed for decades of manipulation and abuse that would continuously benefit the U.S. empire and disadvantage islanders. In nineteen one, a major Supreme Court decision, *Downes v. Bidwell*, ruled that the U.S. Constitution does not necessarily extend its protections and provisions to U.S. territories such as Puerto Rico. *Downes* states that Puerto Rico is not fit to become a state and should thus instead be an unincorporated territory that is not a part of but belongs to the U.S., Puerto Rico is a U.S. possession. This decision made by the Supreme Court in *Downes v. Bidwell* still stands, which puts Puerto Rico in a bit of a quagmire. Even though residents are subject to U.S. rule, the U.S. constitution does not fully protect them, and they do not have Congressional representation. Additionally, according to author and journalist Ed Morales, the Fiscal Oversight and Management Board, or FOMB, has made local Puerto Rican officials essentially powerless, making the possibility of economic self-determination very challenging (6).

The FOMB was established by ex-president Barack Obama in twenty sixteen. The FOMB, referred to by the Puerto Rican people as *La Junta*, represents the Puerto Rican administration in bankruptcy court and makes all budgetary decisions. A bit ironic considering the FOMB, for the most part, contained conservative members connected to the financial sector, some of whom were associated with financial institutions responsible for accruing debt (Morales 2019, 149-150). Because the FOMB makes all major Puerto Rican financial decisions, it is evident the Puerto Rican political agency is a fallacy with the island's administration being more of a face than a functioning body of influence that can enact serious and lasting sociopolitical and financial change.

Another landmark legislature that has contributed to Puerto Rico's oppression is the Merchant Marine Act of 1920, known as the Jones Act, the law that granted U.S. citizenship to Puerto Ricans. The Jones Act established a resident commissioner and a nonvoting representative of Congress, and it subjected the island to its shipping laws, which permanently raised the prices of goods shipped to the island (Morales 2019, 28). Among other things, under the Jones Act, the U.S. could impose tariffs on Puerto Rican trade while its newly established free-trade-zone allowed the U.S. to avoid import duties, making all imports from Puerto Rico to the U.S. duty-free. Only ships constructed in the U.S., flying an American flag, could dock at Puerto Rico's ports, and the act established a triple-tax exemption from the sale of government bonds (Morales 2019, 30). The Jones Act is an exploitative policy premised on the notion that Puerto Rico is not self-determining and must accept rules established by a benevolent guardian force.

Despite the evidence that the U.S. has greatly contributed to, if not initiated, Puerto Rico's debt crisis, the U.S. government has repeatedly disavowed any responsibility for Puerto Rico's precarious financial and political situation. Consequently, Puerto Rico's debt crisis has been greatly misconstrued with many, including ex-President Donald Trump, arguing that the fault lies on the island's corrupt and incompetent government. The argument that the U.S. has no responsibility in Puerto Rico's debt crisis is based on the same colonialist and racist discourse used to justify the U.S.'s mistreatment and abuse of Puerto Rico and its people. The fact is exploitative industrialization efforts followed U.S. colonization and are thus at the root of Puerto Rico's current debt crisis (Morales 2019, 9-10). This industrialization was, rather condescendingly, called Operation Bootstrap. Operation Bootstrap incentivized outside corporations to establish themselves on the island by making the process tax-free and allowing these corporations to employ Puerto Rican residents for less than the minimum wage. As the island industrialized, its natural resources and potential agricultural markets which could have made independence more feasible, continued to deplete, and while these corporations provided jobs, they were not secure, and the pay was inadequate. Refusing to accept U.S. responsibility in Puerto Rico's debt crisis demonstrates a clear ignorance of the effects of U.S. industrialization efforts on the island.

In nineteen ninety-six, the situation for American corporations on the island became less beneficial thanks to the rescinding of a provision of the IRS tax code that provided American corporations with tax breaks. Thus, from nineteen ninety-six to two thousand and six, corporations fled the island, leaving it in a recession (Morales 2019, 10). This led the Puerto Rican government to exacerbate its existing debt, accrued trying to cover essential services, by getting involved with Wall Street municipal bond market speculators (Morales 2019, 10), thus initiating the current seventy-two billion debt crisis and the ludicrousness of arguing that the U.S. is not responsible for Puerto Rican debt.

Protest in Puerto Rico

The only way the Puerto Rican people can hope to achieve any kind of change is through political protest because of the corrupt administration that was instilled through colonialism. Puerto Rico's colonial administration has continuously repressed efforts to further the cause of Puerto Rican independence and self-determination. This is exemplified in the nineteen forty-eight Law 53, known as the Gag Law. The Gag Law prohibited supporting Puerto Rican independence in any form. The law made it illegal to display the Puerto Rican flag as well as sing, play, write, or speak about anything concerning Puerto Rican patriotism and independence. It was a clear effort to suppress the Puerto Rican independence movement. The law was repealed in nineteen fifty-seven, nine years later, on the grounds that it was unconstitutional.[1]

Protest has historically been used by weaker groups to take on the powerful. The Young Lords, the Black Panthers and the Black community during the civil rights movement, the Street Transvestite Action Revolutionaries, the Women's Rights Movement, and the LGBTQ+ community during the first Christopher Street Liberation Day march are all examples of minority groups who effectively confronted their oppressor through protest. The Puerto Rican people are also an example of a weaker group that has taken on their rulers. Prime examples of Puerto Rican political protest and independence efforts include El Grito de Lares (The Cry of Lares) in eighteen sixty-eight, the Rio Piedras Massacre in nineteen thirty-five, and the Ponce Massacre in nineteen thirty-seven, all protests turned tragedy by police brutality. There is also the more recent situation with Vieques, a smaller island that is part of Puerto Rico that used to house a U.S. naval base. While the Puerto Rican people were vehemently opposed to the presence of the base, the government did nothing about removing it until massive protests began in nineteen ninety-nine.

Puerto Rico has been employing protest to object to imperialistic rule since before the United States took hold of the island in the Spanish American War of 1898. In eighteen sixty-eight, what is arguably the most iconic revolt against Spanish rule occurred in Lares, Puerto Rico. El Grito de Lares, The Cry of Lares. Hundreds of rebels looted businesses and offices owned by Spanish-born men in an attempt to combat Spain's exploitative treatment of the Puerto Rico people. The rebels managed to take the Lares city hall but were shut down the next day before they could take control of the next town. While this insurrection was shut down swiftly, its efforts along with Cuba's concurrent struggle for independence, prompted Spain to grant reforms it had continuously denied the islands. Then, in nineteen thirty-five, the University of Puerto Rico became a battleground. Pro-nationalist students who supported Pedro Albizu Campos, the leader of the Puerto Rican Nationalist Party, and his argument that the Chancellor of the university, Carlos E. Chardón, selected by U.S.-appointed governor Theodore Roosevelt Jr, was trying

---

1. 1 Law 53 was repealed when it was declared unconstitutional as it violated American citizens' right to freedom of speech within Article II of the Constitution of Puerto Rico and the First Amendment of the Constitution of the United States.

to turn the university into an institution of American propaganda clashed with students who supported Chancellor Chardón. The Chancellor requested the governor send armed police officers. Four supporters of the Nationalist party and one bystander were killed. Police chief Colonel Elisha Francis Riggs, who was considered responsible for the massacre by Nationalists, was assassinated the following year. The men responsible were Nationalists Hiram Rosado and Elías Beauchamp. Rosado and Beauchamp were arrested and taken to police headquarters in San Juan where officers killed them without a trial. Puerto Rican Senator Luis Muñoz Marín was in D.C. at the time. When asked by the administrator of the Puerto Rico Reconstruction Administration to denounce Riggs' assassination, Muñoz Marín refused unless he could also denounce the police that murdered members of the Nationalist party without giving them a fair trial. Two years later in nineteen thirty-seven, the Puerto Rican Nationalist Party organized a peaceful march to commemorate the abolition of slavery by the Spanish government in Puerto Rico, which occurred in eighteen seventy-three, as well as to protest the imprisonment of Pedro Albizu Campos, the party's leader. The march turned into a violent shooting that claimed the lives of nineteen civilians and two police officers. The United States Commission on Civil Rights investigated the incident and determined that the U.S.-appointed governor of Puerto Rico, Blanton Winship, was responsible for the massacre. Neither the governor nor the policemen who admitted to being involved in the shooting were castigated or prosecuted. However, an independent and collaborative investigation conducted by the United States Commission on Civil Rights, led by Arthur Garfield Hays of the American Civil Liberties Union, and Puerto Rican citizens concluded that the incident was indeed a massacre resulting from mob police brutality and that the governor was responsible for gross civil rights violations. As a result of the Ponce massacre, a chapter of ACLU opened in Puerto Rico. *La Asociación Puertorriqueña de Libertades Civiles.*

Performance as Resistance

The Puerto Rican *cuir* community has spent their lives
resisting not only colonial but also sexual oppression. The
Puerto Rican *cuir* community was politically active before
María—they were engaged in the fight for equal rights and
equal treatment. Thus, Roselló's corrupt and homophobic
behavior was just another item to add to the list of wrongs
that needed to be righted. In other words, the Puerto Rican
cuir community was already well-versed in political activism
and protesting an oppressive administration.

Musical Puerto Rican artists such as Residente, Bad
Bunny, Ricky Martin, and La iLe as well as their politically
active and aware fanbase—composed of everyone from sea-
soned academics to millennials and Puerto Rican youth—
heavily participated in the protests of twenty nineteen. This
demonstrates exactly how music functions as resistance and a
mobilizing force. These artists took to social media to
encourage the Puerto Rican people to show up and protest,
which resulted in massive turnouts. These artists created
music with fierce sociopolitical commentary that speaks to
the Puerto Rican experience, and when the protests against
the Puerto Rican administration erupted, they used their
music to mobilize and fuel the populace.

Residente, Bad Bunny, and La iLe's co-produced song
"Afilando Cuchillos" is the perfect example of politically
conscious music. The artists wrote the song in response to
Ricardo Roselló and the damning chat that the Center for
Investigative Journalism released to the public, and it turned
into an unofficial anthem for those invested in the cause. The
artists accused the ex-governor of sexism, homophobia, corruption, idiocy, and more.

Music was key to the twenty nineteen Puerto Rico protests—not only because of the participation and compositions
of artists such as Bad Bunny, Residente, and La iLe, but also
because of the use of music in physical manifestations such
as the Perreo Combativo (Combative Dance protest), the
Drag Ball, and the massive march on July nineteenth when
the Puerto Rican people made ample use of instruments and
chanting. Residente, Bad Bunny, and La iLe's song as well as

the music and chanting employed by protesters were a mobilizing force with great dramatic and even important short-
term impact. The march of July nineteenth, twenty nineteen,
was the largest in recent history with more than a million
people participating. After the march, then-governor Roselló
finally succumbed to the people's demands and retired from
his post. This was certainly a great accomplishment.

Unfortunately, after the governor stepped down, the
spectacle of protest waned, and so the momentum for protest
was lost. One of the interviewees said as much when she argued
that many were only participating in protests for the fun of it, taking it as an opportunity to party and create chaos. This realization
dawned on her when, during large-scale demonstrations, people
drunkenly hooted and hollered at her, clearly amused by her cuir-
ness and not the sociopolitical critique her drag performance was
trying to convey. Chapter four, Gassed in Drag, takes up these
themes. The central character attends a protest in political
drag and is disappointed when fellow attendees are more
amused by than in sync with her performative protest.

The fear that the general populace did not truly care
about enacting lasting change was realized when the Puerto
Rican people elected as governor a career politician from the
same political party, the New Progressive Party, as Ricardo
Roselló. While all the prominent political parties in Puerto
Rico have engaged in some form of corruption at some point,
the New Progressive Party was caught red-handed and still
reelected.

Despite the Puerto Rican people voting for the same
thing during the last election in twenty, a silver lining of the
recent election was the increase in support for candidates outside of the two most powerful parties—the New Progressive
Party (PNP) and the Popular Democratic Party (PPD) which
have historically maintained administrative power in Puerto
Rico.[1] According to data from the Puerto Rico State Commission of Elections, thirty five point fifty two percent of voter
support was for parties outside of the PNP and PPD in
twenty, a significant increase from the nineteen point thirty-
three percent received in the twenty sixteen elections. This
suggests that the Puerto Rican people are starting to think differently. The younger generation, specifically, is turning to

other parties and candidates who agree there needs to be drastic administrative change in order for progress to occur.

Because the LGBTQIA+ community is no stranger to resisting oppression, it is no wonder they form such a great component of Puerto Rico's post-María activism. For the *cuir* community in Puerto Rico, drag performance not only creatively voices an argument against the unjust sociopolitical status and treatment of the island and its inhabitants, but additionally creates a *cuir*-friendly space where like-minded and like-oppressed non-heteronormative Puerto Rican youth can congregate, exist, and organize. According to transwoman and drag performer Adi Love, Drag performance is about inclusion, it's about celebrating differences, different bodies, different ways of thinking, different identities. My character is the queen of ratchet couture because it's something different. As a woman, people expect you to act and look a certain way. My character is a commentary on this expectation, which is tough for cisgender women, but doubly so for transgender women who have to fight five, six times harder in the eyes of society to measure up.

At Love's performances, the colonially marked *cuir* can exist, heal, and celebrate their difference safely. Thus, these are spaces of *cuir* resistance.

Disidentification and Cuir Controversies

Cuir Puerto Rican drag performance often celebrates difference by satirizing normative culture, this plays an active role in their performance resistance practices. Therefore, Puerto Rican *cuir* performance can be considered a disidentificatory practice. In his work, queer theorist José Esteban Muñoz defines disidentification as a mode of dealing with

---

1. 1 According to the Puerto Rico State Commission of Elections, in the 2020 elections, the PNP and the PPD raked in 32.93% and 31.56% of the votes, while Alexandra Lúgaro (independent runner), the Puerto Rican Independence Party (PIP), and Proyecto Dignidad (a party founded in 2019) acquired 14.21%, 13.72%, and 6.90% of the votes (a final

independent runner accrued .69%).

dominant ideology that works to reform the social norm. Muñoz argues that disidentification is meant to be descriptive of the survival strategies the minority subject practices in order to negotiate a phobic majoritarian sphere that continuously elides or punishes the existence of subjects who do not conform to the phantasm of normative citizenship (2013, 4). He explores disidentification through the analysis of various drag and queer performers whose decision to disidentify has much to do with their sense of identity.

Queer performer Vaginal Crème Davis employs disidentificatory practices in her work. Using disidentificatory performance practices, Davis, a queer of color, managed to become part of the whitewashed LA punk scene (Muñoz 95). Davis disidentifies with commercial drag as much as she disidentifies with the punk scene that rejects her. Instead of attempting to imitate femininity, Davis engages in a *terrorist drag* which stirs up desires and enables subjects to imagine a way of breaking away from the restraint of the social body (Muñoz 100). Davis' drag uses parody and humor to disrupt the social fabric and can thus be considered a disidentificatory strategy with sociopolitical implications (Muñoz 2013, 100).

The performances of *cuir* performer Adi Love approximate Davis' terrorist drag and embody Munoz's concept of disidentificatory practices. Love has greatly helped popularize and expand drag culture in the San Juan metro area of Puerto Rico. Love has an affinity for the grotesque and disturbing, a commentary on the polished and supposed effeminate effect drag should aspire to. Love often employs a prosthetic penis in her performances as well as fake cocaine, blood, and personalized mixes tailored to the theme of her performances. She goes by the name of La Fashion Puelka, the Fashion Pig. Adi's aesthetic is gross, glam, ratchet parody. Drag is all at once Love's ultimate form of expression, self-authentication, and resistance against Puerto Rico's patriarchal, heteronormative society.

Love's drag performances are a political form of disidentifying with communities which she is a part of, Puerto Rican and LGBTQIA+ communities, despite their rejection of her authentic self. Love has had issues with the mainstream drag scene. According to Love,

"Most drag in the queer community, if not all of it, is political because even if you're not talking about a specific topic in politics or being overtly political, drag when done by queer people is political because our existence is political, it's a revolution . . . taking the time to talk about identity is a political statement, and a trans person hitting the stage is a political statement because it is not the norm. Even in the LGBTQIA+ community trans identity is not as represented as it should be. Diversity needs to be represented. Inclusivity needs to be represented. To me, honestly, all queer drag is political, but I have to make the distinction of queer. I'm not saying that a cisgender gay person performing a ballad, or a Madonna song isn't revolutionary, it's drag, it's always meant to be a statement, I just think it's a different level of depth and of being vocally political when you're a queer individual with a different gender identity who's not cisgender or a person of color. I do have to make that distinction because even though I like to think we are all part of the same community, it feels like there's a separation between what's known as the gay community and queer people."

The mainstream drag scene is dominated by cisgender gay drag queens, many of which stick to a pageant aesthetic, hence the term *pageant queen* in the drag world. The fact that Love is a trans woman has caused many of the island's more traditional cisgender drag performers to disregard her. According to Love, this is a common experience for non-binary and trans performers. These cisgender performers invalidate alternative queerness believing there is no point to drag if it is not imitation. For the pageant queen, what's the point of a trans woman doing female drag?

Love's performance can be understood as connected to broader, transnational traditions of drag as activism. Groups created post-Stonewall such as the Street Transvestite Action Revolutionaries, STAR, formed by Sylvia Rivera and Marsha P. Johnson in New York City, and the Sisters of Perpetual Indulgence, started in San Francisco in the late nineteen seventies and now a global organization, have been using drag performance to fight for vulnerable LGBT groups, including homeless drag queens and queer runaways, including the transgender women they advocated for, though this was in an era that predates the language we now use for trans and gender-nonconforming people (Godfrey 2015). In Puerto Rico, the potent and confrontational art of drag is being used not only to further the LGBTQIA+ cause but also to protest the sociopolitical and economic hellscape caused by both the Puerto Rican and U.S. administrations. Thus, drag performers on the island have taken up the revolutionary mantle for all people affected by the current economic and sociopolitical situation, not just the *cuir* community.

Conclusion

In '20, Puerto Rico and its *cuir* community were faced with yet another challenge. COVID-19. Puerto Rico remains in recovery from a number of devastating events, the hurricane, the protests and the ex-governor stepping down, earthquakes, and now the COVID-19 pandemic. This was a blow to all *cuir* performers on the island, who, as COVID-19 forced the shut down on performance spaces, in the blink of an eye lost their entire source of revenue. Once again, these *cuir* individuals had to find a way to survive. *Cuir* Puerto Rican artists took to social media platforms, such as Facebook and Instagram, creating live virtual events such as drag shows, DJ sets, make-up tutorials, interviews, and informational symposiums. Through the use of virtual tip jars and event tickets, performers like Adi Love were able to continue working and providing for themselves. Chapter nine, The Show Must Go On, represents one of these virtual events through Love's perspective.

Love has participated in virtual events dedicated to trans awareness and queer rights issues, demonstrating that the fight did not stop with the protests and eradication of ex-governor Roselló. The fight has just begun, especially for the trans community on the island which continues to face lethal transphobia on a daily basis. This is yet another example of the Puerto Rican *cuir* community's resilience and evidence of their continued efforts to gain acceptance, fair treatment, and ameliorate the island's crippled sociopolitical and economic situation.

The Puerto Rican *cuir* community has been able to rise amid closures and the pandemic precisely for the same reason it was optimally prepared to lead the charge against ex-governor Ricardo Roselló during the protests of the summer of twenty nineteen. The *cuir* community was forged through a life of subjugation. I am a proud, *cuir*, Puerto Rican woman, and as such, my work, like the performances it celebrates, is an act of resistance that protests Puerto Rico's continued colonial treatment, promotes LGBTQIA+ rights, and articulates the power of performative protest. Puerto Rico is part of an international struggle of resistance. It is just one of many countries under oppressive rule. Consequently, this is not just a Puerto Rican issue. It is a global issue of social justice and civil rights which should be of the utmost importance to anyone who believes that all people are indeed created equal.

References

1 Adi Love (drag performer) in discussion with the author, July 18, 2020.

2 Godfrey, Chris. "When Drag is Activism." *The Advocate*, November 4, 2015,
http://www.advocate.com/current-issue/2015/11/04/when-drag-activism.

3 Jhoni Jackson (small business owner) in discussion with the author, July 18, 2020.

4 "La Comay – El Perreo Intenso." La Bemba. July 26, 2019. Video.
https://youtu.be/1ddUmTu_Q7E.

5 Morales, Ed. *Fantasy Island: Colonialism, Exploitation, and the Betrayal of Puerto a'Rico*. New York: Hachette Book Group and Blackstone Publishing, 2019.

6 Muñoz, José Esteban. *Disidentifications: Queers of Color and the Performance of Politics*. Minneapolis: University of Minnesota Press,

2013.

7 Victoria Alejandra Cepeda in discussion with the author, August 20, 2020.

About the Author

Lizbette Ocasio-Russe is currently an Assistant Professor of English at Texas A&M University, Corpus Christi. She completed her Ph.D. in Humanities at the University of Texas at Dallas, her MA in English Literature from the University of Puerto Rico, Rio Piedras campus, and her BA in Journalism and minor in Creative Writing from New York University. She's been published in *Confluence: Journal of Graduate Liberal Studies*, *Flash Fiction Magazine*, *eTropic electronic journal of studies in the tropics*, *postScriptum: An Interdisciplinary Journal of Literary Studies*, *Poui: The Cavehill Journal of Creative Writing*, *Moko: Caribbean Arts and Letters*, and *Tonguas: Student Literary and Artistic Expression Journal*. Lizbette also has a short fiction story that will be published in the 9th edition of *Writing Texas*. \

Bringing Rainbow Stories to Life

Visit us at our website: www.flashpointpublications.com